Sherlock Holmes
on the
Western Front

By the same author

Sherlock Holmes
on the
Western Front

Val Andrews

**BREESE
BOOKS
LONDON**

First published in 2000 by
Breese Books Ltd
164 Kensington Park Road, London W11 2ER, England

ISBN: 0 947 533 87 7

Typeset in 11½/14pt Caslon by
Ann Buchan (Typesetters), Middlesex
Printed and bound in Great Britain by
Itchen Printers Ltd, Southampton

CHAPTER ONE

A Plea for Help

It was a bright spring morning in 1916 that I found myself walking briskly through St James's Park, revelling in this brief respite from any sign of the dreadful combat in which our country was involved. The ducks appeared to be unconcerned regarding the events which affected even their normally uneventful lives, but, did I imagine it or were the starlings keeping an ever-watchful lookout for Zeppelins or air-machines? As I turned into the streets again the patriotic posters and khaki-clad passersby brought it all back.

It had been a terrible two years; opening with that foolish note of 'over by Christmas' optimism. At first Londoners had scarcely noticed the war at all and I confess I had been as over-confident as the next man, my thoughts filled with expectations of a quick push on the Western Front followed by the Kaiser begging for terms. Alas, this had not happened and the trenches of the allies and the Germans had presented a deadlock save where the French had an alarming amount of their border overrun. Strategic position had changed back and forth with monotonous regularity, but at a terrifying toll in human life. The journalists had kept up their patriotic jingoism and the cartoonists had continued to depict the Kaiser as either a buffoon or a horrific monster. Invalid soldiers in hospital blue had begun to give a dazed public some idea of what was really happening on the Western Front and a certain amount of grumbling, quite uncharacteristic in the British, could be encountered. There were even those who opined the unbelievable idea that France and Britain might have to come to some sort of agreement with the Kaiser, ideas that could have had them arrested at the time, but of which I can now speak freely.

Any regular reader of mine will hardly need to be told that I had volunteered for military service as soon as I had realized that there was a shortage of experienced medical officers. However, having had my own version of my age disbelieved by half a dozen examining MOs I eventually had to give up all thoughts of actual participation.

Imagine, then, my surprise at being asked eventually for my participation at a stage when I had all but given up hope. It happened in a rather surprising way and from an unexpected quarter. But I am getting ahead of myself in this narration, so let me return to that stroll through London during that war that was to end all wars. I reached my goal, the Diogenes Club. I had, to my surprise, been summoned to meet Mycroft, the brother of my friend and colleague Mr Sherlock Holmes.

Watson, my dear fellow, pray be seated and I will ring for refreshments.'

I had not seen Mycroft for quite a few years, for since Sherlock had retired to keep bees in Sussex I had not had reason for contact. But there he was, much the same, though perhaps just a trifle stouter. He said, 'You are looking well,' but that seemed to be the extent of his niceties of conversation. He leapt straight into his reason for our meeting.

'You see, Watson, I have tried to get Sherlock to come here to see me on a matter of national importance, but he flatly refuses to budge from that wretched retreat of his near Eastbourne or wherever it is. However, you are much closer to him than I am, despite our being blood relatives, and don't bother to deny it because it is true. Now, for you he would come here, if you were to request it of him. Why, man, you have managed to get him away from that wretched place on a number of occasions during the past decade. Please tell me that you will do your best.'

I realized that I was placed in a very awkward situation. I had always, since his retirement, respected Holmes's privacy knowing how he hated anything smacking of a return to his old life as an investigator interrupting his rural activities. Yet here was a man who not only enjoyed the confidence of the British government, but on occasions *was* the British government, making a request of me that appeared to have some kind of urgency. I had to be sure.

'Please, can you, or rather are you, in a position to tell me the nature of the urgent matter involved? You see, I too would have the greatest difficulty in prising him away from his retreat, and those occasions which you speak of were not managed easily.'

Mycroft Holmes breathed hard and deep, crossed one elegantly trousered leg over the other and removed the cigar from his mouth. 'My dear Watson, I need hardly tell you that our country is in grave danger. The newspapers obviously cannot be expected to keep all the bad news from the public but, take it from me, the picture is far, far more gloomy than they can be permitted to present. We are presently engaged in a life-and-death struggle with a deadly, dangerous foe, far better prepared, armed and motivated than ourselves.' (He glanced around him and lowered his voice.) 'Watson, we could conceivably lose this conflict.'

I gasped with all but disbelief. 'But dash it man, we are British and moreover our army has the collaboration of our great and noble allies, the French. Between us we have held the Germans on the Western Front for two years or more. It is only a matter of time before we make one big advance between us that will not only drive the Hun back but make him retreat in great disorder.'

Mycroft paused for a moment before he replied, 'Oh Watson, I can see that you have little idea of the real position. Yes, we are British and we have, or had, a first-class army and a renowned navy and have conquered over the past hundred years all but half the world. But those armies that we beat were for the most part poorly armed hordes of simple native peoples. Look what happened when we came up against the Boers; a lightly armed but sophisti-cated guerrilla force. Oh yes, we won both of the Boer wars, but only after much trial and error and ultimately only through vast superiority of numbers. As for the French, yes they are a famed fighting force but they seem to know little more than we do about fighting such a well-armed and motivated foe. They don't have the stomach for it Watson. They have lost at least a million soldiers and, unlike us, they have had part of their country trampled by the spurred boots of the Germans. I warn you, my friend, there is a genuine danger of the French making a separate peace with the Prussians!'

I was horrified at his words. 'What! The French capitulate and leave us to fight alone? Never!' (His words had not only troubled, but angered me.) 'Do you realize, Mycroft, that there is a new bylaw against such defeatest talk?'

'Realize it, Watson? Why, I drafted it. Please, I am the most patriotic of men, but in confiding in you I am bound to tell the truth. There is a ray of hope in the possibility that America may eventually enter the conflict on our side, of course. With their vast resources and huge population they could raise an army that would save the day. I am, of course, working my fingers to the bone to bring this life-saving circumstance nearer to probability.'

I stifled a chuckle, turning it into a diplomatic cough, this caused by a mental picture of a man who in years had scarce left his club chair working his fingers, or any other part of his vast anatomy, to the bone. But of course what he had told me had been no joke. I had known that the war news was not encouraging, yet had not realized its gravity.

'Mycroft, what can I do to help? I am my King's man, I will do whatever my country needs me to do.'

He nodded and then smiled hugely, 'Good man! Well, Watson, I will tell you what you must do. You must go to this place in Sussex and bring your friend, my brother, here to me. I know what has to be done but I am not physically capable of bringing it about. Sherlock is but two and sixty by my calculations and fit as that wretched fiddle of his. You know what I mean, fencing and boxing and all that!'

'He suffers with arthritis.'

'Does he indeed? Well, he will have to overcome all that;

his country needs him, he has no time for aches and pains. Do your duty, Watson. Fetch Sherlock Holmes.'

The housekeeper showed me to the sitting-room at the rear of Holmes's delightful Sussex farmhouse. As I entered the room I perceived the back of his head as he sat in a high-backed chair facing the open french windows.

Before the lady could announce me he spoke in those incisive tones that I knew so well. 'My dear Watson, pray enter, I have been expecting you. So you have not managed to hoodwink the army concerning your age or mobility?'

'How did you know that I was coming here to see you, or that I had even contemplated joining the army, let alone having been turned down?'

'Oh, come Watson, Mycroft has been writing, sending telegrams, messengers with official "orders" imploring me to go to London and consult with him. It was only a matter of time before he blackmailed you into coming to badger me. As for your attempts to join the army, my knowledge of your patriotic character would make that obvious. Likewise my knowledge of your physical condition would tell me that they would turn you down. We are much of an age, you and I; we must leave the conduct of the war to others, younger and fitter than ourselves.'

I was a little surprised and disappointed with his attitude. I remonstrated, appealing to his sense of patriotism without touching on any of the extreme worries that Mycroft had conveyed to me. But then to my amazement I scarcely needed to dwell upon those dangers about which I had been warned, for he seemed more than well aware of them.

Holmes continued, 'If the leaders of this great nation, of which you and I have so long been respectable, law-abiding, tax-paying citizens, cannot manage its affairs on our behalf in a more sensible manner they have no right to blackmail us into trying to get them out of the trouble into which its pompous diplomats and soldiers have landed them. In the words of Lord Clive, "We have shown the state some service". No, Watson, their stupidity has landed us in a war which it seems we cannot win. Let them find the way out!'

We sat at the antique dining table whilst Holmes attempted to be a generous host. But, unfortunately, his household seemed as short of those little luxuries which make life worth living as any other war-weary ménage. He demanded meat but we got toasted cheese on bread. This was followed by a concoction which Mrs MacDonald, the housekeeper, referred to as Lord George Pudding. It appeared to be a sort of fruit roll with carrots and honey replacing the usual fruit and sugar. I had grown used to such things but Holmes evidently found it difficult to come to gastronomic terms with any such compromise. We washed it down with some cider which we drank from stone mugs. Holmes looked at the good woman with an expression which said, 'Tell me there is a war on just once more and I will explode!'

Later we strolled among the beehives and I was interested to note that the pleasant garden which led down to the apiary had been converted to grow potatoes and beans. Holmes tried to behave as if the vegetable patch did not exist and that the lavender bushes and flowering plants were still present as they had been on my last visit.

Then a diversion occurred in the shape of a postman on a

bicycle who had brought the mail from the village. The letters were on a small table beside Holmes's armchair when we returned to the sitting-room.

There were three items and Holmes inspected them and told me that which they contained without recourse to opening them. 'The first envelope contains a bill from the gas company; I recognize the particularly revolting-looking buff envelope. The company in their wisdom evidently changed their minds regarding how much to charge me for you will observe that the envelope has been opened and resealed. They have decided to charge me more rather than less.'

I said nothing, I simply irritated him by ignoring his deduction to the point that he felt forced to explain. 'You see, Watson, if I have overpaid it is their habit to enclose a credit slip. As this is of some value they would have felt bound to either reseal the envelope with gummed paper or provide a fresh envelope.' He opened the container with a paper-knife. 'As I surmised, an alteration but not in my favour.'

'What is inside the other envelope?' (I had decided to surrender.)

'Oh, it is from some ministry of this or that; betrayed by the crown printed on the back flap. It is in fact from the ministry that concerns itself with agriculture and is something in the form of a questionnaire, sent to a great many persons in this area. This can be determined by the fact that they have had to engage temporary or emergency staff to cope with the scale of their bureaucracy. You will see how the envelope has been addressed in a careless fashion, omitting to write the word "esquire" after my name. Moreover, the stamp has been stuck upon the envelope at an angle; something which no professional clerk would do.'

He ripped it open impatiently. 'As I surmised, Watson, I am asked to fill in what they refer to as an "application to keep livestock in wartime". This means that they have observed my hives and want to get their thieving hands upon my honey!'

Sherlock Holmes paced the sitting-room and muttered to himself, treating me as if I did not exist. This pacing and muttering continued for some minutes. Then he seated himself and filled a calabash from the turkish slipper which had survived his transportation from Baker Street. He lit it with a vesta and fixed me with his gimlet eyes. 'Watson, the world is going quite mad. We are in deep as we discussed, and what Mycroft believes that I could possibly do to extricate our country from its problem I know not. However, I refuse to fill in these petty little slips of paper and the sooner they run out of excuses for sending them to me the better. No need to look up a suitable train for they run upon each hour from Brighton to Victoria. Be so good as to ask Mrs Hudson to send Billy for a cab.'

Of course, I knew that he meant for me to ask Mrs MacDonald to send George for such a vehicle, so I did not bother to point out his mistake. I was just happy to have fulfilled my mission and only hoped that Sherlock Holmes could help to save his country. I had no reason to see how he could, but then who would have thought that he could have saved Sir Henry Baskerville from the effects of a curse in which many believed.

Holmes decided to put up at the Charing Cross Hotel and quite refused to go to the Diogenes Club to see Mycroft.

'You must go there and fetch my lazy brother, Watson, that is if you think he might take that amount of trouble. Perhaps he might care to arrange for us to dine with him at Simpson's; assuming that it has not closed for the duration like so many other establishments.'

I reassured him that Simpson's was still operating, although with a greatly curtailed menu.

He was relieved to hear this and continued, 'It is not mere selfishness on my part, dragging Mycroft away from the Diogenes in only about the second or third time in living memory. No, there is method in my audacious suggestion. You see, the Diogenes is so well known as Mycroft's lair that I feel elsewhere might be better for reasons of secrecy.'

Considering that it was wartime, the meal was excellent, although I did forgo the Lloyd George Pudding! (Holmes declared it to be adequate.) The gentlemen of the orchestra were all evidently serving in various military bands, but the quartet of lady musicians did their best. The head waiter (fortunately beyond military age) was delighted to see Holmes again after a number of years and produced for us a bottle of sparkling French wine, to the envy of other diners who had to make do with English substitutes which I knew from experience were really a sort of disguised cider.

Mycroft looked around him eventually to be sure that we were quite alone, then leaned his huge bulk forward in his chair, lowering his voice to little more than a whisper. 'Sherlock, the matter is extremely serious; the war could be lost if we do not pull our socks up. Our French allies are practically exhausted, having lost an unbelievable number of soldiers on the Western Front. Of course, they are good chaps but hardly a match for the Germans on their own. We are doing our best, as you know, but our numbers, despite conscription, are strictly limited and it would take the intervention of the Americans on the allied side to really settle the matter. With their huge population their army could be a godsend, and they have the wherewithal to equip it. They could turn the balance in our favour. We are tired out as a nation, Sherlock, though not to the state suffered by the French.'

Holmes had listened carefully, but seemed puzzled as to where his own influence could be brought into play, saying, 'My dear Mycroft, I have very little influence with our American cousins. Perhaps you should be talking to our friend Miss Irene Adler; she is enterprising indeed. Seriously though, there must be some other aspect which makes you believe that I can be of use.'

Mycroft lit a corona after having explained how difficult it was getting to obtain them. But he did then come to the long-awaited point of our meeting. 'Sherlock, the Germans are running rings around our secret service and they seem to know our intended troop movements almost as fast as the orders are issued. I tell you, the Western Front is, in consequence, becoming a shambles. We have only been able to prevent a much deeper invasion of France and Belgium by the sheer grit and bravery of our chaps. Imagine having to go over the top only to be greeted by a force that has obviously been alerted to the plan.'

'Tell me, how are these orders to attack given, and by whom?'

'Mostly the local commander issues the orders, having received his own from higher authority, and these days most orders are issued by field telephone rather than the old-style runners.'

'I see. So there is not just the chance of the telephone wires being tapped but infiltration by spies, around these higher authorities, even near to the Commander-in-Chief himself.'

'We are vigilant, Sherlock, but of course the situation is so bad that almost anything is possible.'

Holmes was thoughtful as he puffed at one of Mycroft's precious cigars. Eventually he spoke and when he did he used words that I had not expected to hear. 'Watson and I will have to go to the Western Front in order to investigate.'

'Too dangerous, dear brother, too dangerous!'

'Oh come, I don't mean that we should go to the trenches themselves; although I do not completely discount the possibility; rather, behind the lines where we stand some sort of chance of survival in order that we might investigate.'

A surge of excitement ran through me. 'By Jove, Holmes, how soon can we leave?'

'My dear Watson, hold your horses. We will have to decide upon some kind of subterfuge first. We must play roles, you and I, which will logically leave us time to observe without creating any suspicion concerning our real task.'

Mycroft looked thoughtful, then he brightened. 'How would it be if we sent you and Watson out to entertain the troops?'

I dropped my coffee cup and a waiter, mopping up the mess that I had caused, prevented Mycroft from immediately enlarging on his suggestion and any possible sense it might hold. But eventually the fellow had cleared up, provided me with a fresh cup and been hastily dismissed.

Mycroft was not only serious, but I suspected that he was just a little amused by his own idea. 'Sherlock is a wonder on the violin and I happen to know that you, Watson, are something of a pianist.'

I gasped; I could not quite believe that Mycroft was being serious. 'In the mess, for a sing-song, yes. But to play seriously, for an audience? You cannot mean what you say, Mycroft!'

'Oh come, Watson, you play quite well enough to accompany Sherlock in the simpler pieces. I have also heard that you were something of a conjurer when you were a student; you can throw in a little sleight of hand. I'll obtain another agent who can sing or dance or something, and we will have a sort of miniature concert party to send behind the lines. Splendid idea. You will be far enough from the trenches to minimize the danger of your being killed, but near enough to learn just what is going on.'

I glanced helplessly at Sherlock, but his reaction did not reassure me. I had expected an instant outburst of refusal; instead, unbelievably, I heard Holmes all but approve of his brother's, to me, outrageous suggestion. 'My dear Mycroft, whilst I do not relish the thought of performing as a violinist at troop concerts I can see the advantages of your suggestion. Watson is too modest, he is well able to provide a piano background, and has quite a repertoire of experiments culled from Hoffman's *Modern Magic.*'

Mycroft was relieved. 'Splendid, it is not as if you will be thrown in at the deep end, you fellows. I'll send you to Salisbury Plain first for a couple of performances nearer home just to get you into the swing of things. Cheer up, Watson, those army-hut pianos are always out of tune: why, on one of them you and Paderewski would sound much the same. I'll set it all up: there's nothing like striking whilst the iron is hot, what? In fact, we had better strike whilst there is still an iron left, if you see what I mean.'

After Mycroft had departed in one of the new motor taxi-cabs for the Diogenes Club, we sat a long time over our final cups of coffee. I tried to tell myself that the events of the past hour had just not occurred and that I was not really going to the Western Front to play the piano. In fact, dear reader, it was like some horrible nightmare.

But Holmes was quite calm and seemed untroubled by the awesome tasks that seemed to have been allotted to us. He sounded in fact quite amused as he said, 'Come, Watson, cheer up. It should not take us long to accomplish our two main tasks.'

'Holmes, I am not sure that I am completely clear what those two tasks might be.'

'First, we must find out how the Germans are intercepting our communications. Second, we must find a way to bring the Americans into the conflict.'

I was intrigued by the way he treated the latter task, throwing it into the conversation almost as an afterthought. What was he planning; to persuade the Kaiser to visit Washington to spit in the face of the American President? I knew from my daily study of the newspapers that many Americans, if not the greater number, considered the European war to be none of their business and would prefer their great country to preserve its neutrality. I failed to see how Holmes could succeed where our diplomats were failing.

I accompanied my old friend to Charing Cross and then took the same cab to my home. Once there, I entered my living-room and cast a rueful eye at the upright piano. The servants were in bed and, loath to awaken them, I made myself a pot of coffee. But awaken them I did because after a while I could not resist the awful temptation of playing a few notes upon the Broadwood. As I tried to render 'Home Sweet Home' my housekeeper burst into the room in her dressing robe, brandishing an umbrella which she, with great presence of mind, had taken from the stand in the hall as she had passed through it. Just behind her was the maid servant, in mob cap and dressing gown, in a state of terror, which strangely contrasted with the housekeeper's air of authority.

'Oh bless me, Doctor, thank goodness it's you!' She lowered the umbrella and relaxed somewhat.

'Mrs Parkin, forgive me. I did not realize that it was quite so loud. I confess I got carried away!'

It is a characteristic of the British that they feel obliged to behave apologetically in front of their servants. Perhaps, I mused, this was why we were in danger of losing the war.

CHAPTER TWO

Preparing for the Fray

I wondered who would call our next meeting and where it might be. I had not long to wonder, because at about noon on the following day Sherlock Holmes casually arrived at my home nonchalantly puffing at his pipe but dressed in clothing uncharacteristic for him. He wore a velvet jacket and a floppy bow tie of considerable proportions.

I said, 'Holmes, it is good to see you as ever but I am somewhat taken aback by your attire. You look for all the world like a musician!'

'My very intention, Watson, I purchased these items from a secondhand shop on my way here.' He raised a paper parcel which hung by its twine from his left hand. 'These are my more usual clothes and I changed that I might try my new attire upon you for a reaction. Your words reassure me.'

He did, then, intend to take on a new identity; this should have occurred to me from the start, and I wondered as to my own change of clothes and personality.

Holmes read my mind as always, saying, 'Oh, I think a

frock-coat and checked trousers for you, Watson, and within a few days you could enlarge your moustache and mutton chops, allowing them to combine into suitably doleful dundrearies to make your disguise complete. I intend to refrain from cutting my hair which will soon give me a suitably artistic appearance, combined with a set of pince-nez!' He fished a pair of such spectacles from his pocket and fastened them onto his prominent nose. I had to admit that with the new jacket and bow they did affect a transformation fit for a fiddler!

Holmes insisted on taking me to a nearby used-clothing shop to select my new wardrobe. He had an unerring eye in such establishments. The frock-coat he selected for me had seen better days but was still respectable enough and was a tolerable fit. The trousers were neat enough and he insisted that I take a paisley-patterned waistcoat to unsuitably set everything off.

So when we repaired to a local hostelry for some bread, cheese and ale it was my turn to be carrying the twine-bound paper package.

Holmes said, 'From this moment I will forsake my pipe in favour of Egyptian cigarettes. They will suit my new character and will be strong enough to relieve my craving for strong narcotics. You are advised to affect something other than that bulldog pipe of yours too, Watson. Most pianists of my experience have smoked virginia cigarettes, and distributed the ash upon their vests. Aye, and managed to burn quite a few piano tops as well.'

When we got back to my house we decided to have a tentative rehearsal. Of course, Holmes had left his Stradivarius back in Sussex, but he explained that he had not intended to take it to France with him. 'My insurance broker would go off his head if I took my violin anywhere other than to a concert hall. I will ask you, with your expert knowledge of the district in which you reside, to steer me to a shop where I might purchase something more suitable for the occasion and character which I must play.'

Fortunately I recalled a shop called Rowland's Musical Emporium where violins old and new were sold, bought and exchanged along with many other assorted instruments.

As we entered through the seedy entrance, Holmes threw back his head and took a deep breath. 'Breathe it in, Watson, that nostalgic air of seasoned wood, resin, leather, dust, damp manuscripts and disinfectant. A second-hand musical instrument shop has a wonderfully exciting aura all of its own.'

As it happened, this particular second-hand instrument shop was well kept for such an establishment. The instruments had been sorted into some kind of order, and each violin for instance was with an appropriate case and bow.

'No bargains to be had here, Watson.'

'What makes you say that?'

'Where the dirt of ages has been cleaned away, the seller expects a fair return for his enterprise. Look at this instrument for example, recently cleaned . . .' He picked up a once handsome but now much scratched and scarred fiddle which lay in an open case. It was marked 'Mellow, £1'. '. . . notice the dust and grime traces which can still be seen beneath the pegs which tune it. Its previous owner neglected it for some years; possibly did not touch it for a decade, indeed had no interest in it whatsoever.'

I began to think that Holmes was using imagination as well as observation and said as such. 'I'll grant you the fact that it was neglected for a long time, but at least he kept it in a case.'

Holmes examined the case carefully and then continued, 'I'll wager by its condition that the instrument was not kept in a case over the past several years.'

'Strange to own a violin that you do not use and not have the sense to store it in its case.'

'True, if its previous owner had a case to put it in.'

I indicated the case from which he had lifted the violin.

He shook his head sadly. 'Really, Watson, I would have thought that you would have noticed that the instrument and the case are entirely unrelated. The violin, if one is to believe the maker's label inside, was made by a Signor Restelli in 1891. It is scarred to show that it remained unprotected until the owner of this establishment found a suitable case which is of an earlier vintage to make it more saleable.'

I glanced inside the case and saw the trademark: C. Schmidt, Vienna. It was undated but by now I was prepared to allow that Holmes was accurate as ever with his deductions. I wondered if he would choose to buy this particular instrument, noting that he was making a quick examination of several others. He tuned a couple of them and played a note or two, but eventually returned to that which had first caught his eye. He tuned and played it. There were one or two browsers in the shop who instantly gave their full attention to Holmes's playing.

The owner of the shop, young Mr Rowland, a man of some five-and-fifty years and son of the founder, rubbed his podgy hands together and smiled craftily. 'An excellent choice, sir, if I might say so. Shall we say two pounds with its bespoke container?'

Holmes drew horsehair over sheep gut in one final high note. He fixed Rowland with an intense gaze. 'Rather shall we say one pound as advertised? The other instruments are marked "with case"; it is inferred that this one is also priced to include that accessory. I assure you, sir, that I might be just a poor musician, but I am not without influence.'

Rowland decided that this was not a customer to be argued with and he accepted the one pound with which he would have been happy had he not heard the instrument played. Its mellow tone had struck a note of greed in him, having believed that the instrument would sound as shoddy as it looked.

That evening Holmes practised upon his newly acquired violin whilst I tried to play a background upon my piano. Eventually we had run through some half-a-dozen pieces which Holmes considered would make a useful repertoire. These included 'Greensleeves', a Strauss waltz or two and some Gilbert and Sullivan. All were light and bright pieces.

'The stuff to give the troops, eh Watson? Now what of your own repertoire for pianoforte solos. Make it varied and use attack.'

I tinkered around upon the ivories, eventually deciding upon modern pieces such as 'Pack Up Your Troubles' and 'Roses of Picardy'.

At length it was puzzled to find enough bright melodies until Holmes came to my rescue, saying, 'Think of those nights at the music hall, Watson. I know that you have been a great supporter of Miss Marie Lloyd and Mr George Robey.'

Instantly I rattled through a selection which included 'If You Were the Only Girl in the World', 'One of the Ruins that Cromwell Knocked About a Bit' and 'The Galloping Major'.

Holmes applauded languidly and said, 'Splendid, my dear fellow, I can see you topping the bill at the Metropolitan or the Oxford yet. But pray do not forget to appear casual, as if used to playing in public houses. Now there is more plotting and planning to be done. We have to invent for ourselves new personas, and backgrounds.'

Holmes decided that he would be known as Sigmund Hailsham and that I should become Jason Wentworth. He a concert violinist whose lack of ability to comply with the discipline of the concert hall had prevented him from becoming a celebrated soloist whilst my own failure to pass certain medical examinations had made me turn to an indifferent musical talent. Of course, the reader will have realized by now that Holmes had decided upon these things entirely on his own and any discussion of them or debate was mere formality.

I did, however, ask one question. 'Holmes, I have just realized that our new names have kept our same initials. Is there any special reason for this?'

'You do not suppose that it is coincidental, do you Watson? No, I have long realized that if you take on a false name some small article in personal use, or a laundry mark bearing initials, can give one away. However careful one is to eliminate such things, oversights can occur. Take the word of an old campaigner.'

As an equally old campaigner myself I opened my mouth to speak but then bit my lip instead and decided to accept being Jason Wentworth, so long as it was not for too long.

This new invention, the telephone, which despite its frequent vicissitudes enables one to quickly contact another within a certain area, is both a blessing and a bother. Holmes had never really take to it but, as a medical man, I had no option but to make use of it. In this instance I found it convenient to be able to send for Holmes's luggage, making another visit to Charing Cross unnecessary. I was also able to telephone the Diogenes Club to inform Mycroft concerning Holmes's domicile with me at my home. Of course, Mycroft found the telephone a boon and a blessing, having for years had to rely upon others to run messages and errands. Now he could actually contact those he wished to confer with without leaving his armchair. 'Should have been invented twenty years earlier!' Well of course it had, but it had only recently become available to more than a handful of people. Now one can ring someone in the West End from a residence in Hampstead, and soon we are promised a network of exchanges to cover the greater part of the British Isles. Although he would not admit it, the system would have been invaluable to Holmes during the years of his professional work as an investigator. For example, if Miss Steiner had been able to telephone Holmes from the village of Stoke Moran she would not have risked being shadowed by her horrific guardian.

My reason for this essay upon telephonic communication is simply to better explain to the reader how we were able to so quickly arrange certain things with Mycroft, and he with others, so that our expedition to the south-west was so easily organized.

We found ourselves upon a train bound for Salisbury,

both of us in character as Messrs Hailsam and Wentworth. Our fellow passengers included many soldiers returning to the myriad army camps that abounded in the area of Salisbury Plain. These camps were, of course, the training centres where the young innocents were prepared for the horrors of the Western Front. There were native English, Scots and Welsh, and a surprising number of Irishmen, plus a smattering of Canadians and other colonials, who, had their uniforms not been varied, could even have been recognized for what they were from their healthier appearance and more outgoing manner of presenting themselves.

We were met at Salisbury by an army sergeant of the old school who did not, however, ask for any credentials of a printed sort, which was as well because we had none (although Mycroft had promised to send us some as soon as his forgers had finished them). I imagine our general appearance seemed proof enough of our identity to the sergeant, who had picked us out in the crowd simply from a superficial description that he had been given.

'You'll be comfortable enough at the White Hart, gents. I'll take you there in the car, and tomorrow afternoon I'll come and fetch you and take you to your first engagement. It's a garrison theatre near Amesbury. After the performance you can stay the night at the camp and I'll take you on to your next place, that's if you do all right tomorrow!'

He laughed, but his laugh was brittle, as if there was an element of truth in what he had said. Normally I would not have doubted it, but of course I knew that even if the soldiers threw things at us there would inevitably be other performances.

We passed through magnificent pine forests as we sat

uncomfortably with our luggage in the small Ford motor-car. (Doubtless built for a quite different market but not liberally daubed with khaki-brown paint.)

Holmes seemed to notice something of interest as he gazed at the trees but he made no comment. Indeed his only communication on the journey was when he asked the sergeant, 'This area is part of a big estate, is it not?'

'Yes, sir. Lord Gorse's place we are on now; commandeered, of course, by the War Department for the duration.'

'His Lordship has recently returned from North America, has he not?'

'Why yes, sir, he got back just before the balloon went up so to speak. Do you know his Lordship?'

'No, I must have read it somewhere in the newspaper.'

Holmes, realizing his mistake in time, was anxious to play down his discussion concerning Lord Gorse. I recognized this and was puzzled by the episode.

The White Hart proved to be pleasant enough and its bedrooms comfortable enough, though spartan as far as the furnishings were concerned. After we had unpacked, which took perhaps five minutes, we repaired to the bar parlour and ordered two tankards of ale. As we were now on our own I expressed my puzzlement with Holmes's hastily subdued remark concerning the travels of Lord Gorse.

He explained, 'One of the disadvantages of an assumed alias is that one has to be careful not to betray oneself with one's normal characteristics. For an unguarded moment I was Sherlock Holmes but fortunately I don't think the sergeant noticed. You see, my deduction was based upon the sight of a grey squirrel which scampered up one of the pine trees.'

I admit that I was still bewildered. 'How could a squirrel shinning up a tree tell you anything of Lord Gorse's itinery?'

'I know this area well, Watson. The pine woods here have naturally long been infested with the bushy-tailed rodents; but of the native variety, which as you know is of the reddish brown sort. The one I saw was a silvery grey.'

A "sport", like a black lamb?'

'No, because it had none of the other characteristics which are usual in our native nut-eater. For instance, its ears were not tufted and it was clearly of a larger breed. It was in fact a North American grey.'

'You infer that Lord Gorse brought it home as a pet? But he might have done that years ago and it could have recently escaped from a cage.'

'I think it more likely that as with some other English landowners he saw the little animals in America and imported a few of them to populate his woodland.'

'Could that not have been some years ago?'

'I doubt it, because I noticed some native red squirrels around, and once the grey is established it quickly expels its English cousins. This will happen within a few months, and Lord Gorse is extremely foolish to have introduced an animal which will soon become a pest. Moreover, the creatures will soon spread throughout the south-west of England if not checked.'

I still had some doubts, feeling that Holmes's powers of deduction might have decreased with age. He had, after all, shown a lack of judgement by his own admission in mentioning the matter of Gorse's American visit in front of the sergeant. However, events would soon occur to dispel these foolish doubts of mine.

We had dinner at the White Hart and it proved to be a wholesome if modest repast. There were cold cuts with boiled potatoes, served with cabbage, broad beans, mushrooms and peas. There followed an equally modest pudding, served with hot treacle. The cheese and bread were doubtless of local origin and were excellent. Of course in the piping days of peace we might have expected better, but we agreed that for wartime the repast was adequate.

Then Holmes pushed his coffee cup aside and said quietly to me, 'Watson, I feel like a walk. Come, let us smuggle our pipes and tobacco out with us and stroll near Stonehenge; it is a year or two since I have viewed it. On the last occasion there were many sightseers, but in wartime it might be very comfortable to stroll around and examine it; that is if it is not upon War Department land.'

We took a road from Amesbury to Shrewton, which Holmes assured me would take us past Stonehenge. He was right, and the strange prehistoric structure came into view when we had been strolling for no longer than forty minutes. There were few persons to be seen; we were passed by a military vehicle or two and a lone farm cart. Then, as dusk began to fall, we got out our pipes and gratefully lit up.

My friend chuckled, 'Does this remind you of indulging in an illicit clay whilst at school, Watson?'

'Indeed it does. Hippo Craig and I used to have an illegal smoke in the box-room at Greyfriars. I cannot tell you how pleasing it is to indulge in proper tobacco again.'

'Quite so, Watson. The cigarettes, even strong Egyptian or black Turkish, can only subdue my craving for this Scottish mixture.'

As for Stonehenge itself, there were no sightseers around

it and despite the gloom of dusk we had a splendid opportunity to examine the stones. I had long been fascinated by its possible origin and original purpose. 'It is megalithic, is it not, Holmes?'

'So they tell us, Watson, so they tell us.'

'You doubt the findings of the celebrated archaeologists and scientists?'

'Oh, I do not exactly doubt that they believe their own findings. But they are still lacking agreement among themselves. For example, they are not completely in accord as to the original purpose of the stones. Some assure us that it is a place of worship, others that it was a burial ground.'

I just felt that I had to air what knowledge I had on the subject. 'I have read that it could have been a place of sacrifice, and that the midsummer rays will strike the heelstone on the dawn of Midsummer's Day. This could indicate that it is a sort of giant sundial, serving as some sort of almanack.'

I should have known that Holmes had more knowledge than I concerning this as well as most other subjects . . .

'A fallacy, Watson! The phenomena that you have described will eventually take place, but it will be all but a thousand years into the future and certainly could not have happened in the conceivable past. Please disregard much that you read in *The Wonderbook of Science.*'

'What, then, do you imagine was its original purpose?'

'I can only conjecture, Watson, that it was a building, of which this is merely the skeleton. The thirty enormous stones which form the main circle have equally wide gaps which were possibly filled in with other brick-like stones or even timber which would have been filched many centuries ago. Indeed the local peasants would have taken the stones which remain had they had the means; their sheer size and weight have saved them for us to ponder. The inner circle of even higher and broader stones indicate that they might have supported a roof of thatch, timber, slate or even less substantial material. It could, after all, have been to support a monster tent. In any case it would guess that it was sort of amphitheatre. The inner circle of smaller, bluish stones is of interest; I recognize them as being peculiar to the Prescelly Hills in south Wales.'

At last I believed I had caught Holmes out in an inexactitide. 'How then could these megalithic people have transported them from Wales? Come, the wheel was not even in use at that time!'

But Holmes was up to the challenge that I had thrown him. 'They were possibly floated on massive rafts, a few at a time, up what we now call the Bristol Channel, and then hauled the last few miles, either by vast horsepower or by enormous numbers of men. But in any case I doubt that they had no sort of primitive wheel. After all, the local stones had to be brought to this spot and they were even larger and of immense weight. They might have been rolled on tree poles to this site.'

As darkness began to descend we sat a short distance from the so-called Druids' circle and enjoyed our smoke. It was a while, perhaps a quarter of an hour, before I noticed a kind of glow from near the foot of one of the vast columns. I mentioned this to Holmes only to realize that he had been studying it himself for a while.

I asked him, 'Could it be some sort of natural phenomenon, such as glow worms?'

'I think not, Watson. Such creatures move and are usually found among hedgerows and shrubs. This is a steady glow, unwinking and emanating from the short grass around the base of one of the stones. I suggest that instead of continuing to conjecture we view it from close quarters.'

We strolled over towards the glow, without urgency in our steps, for we had no reason to suspect anything unworldly or sinister. It turned out to be a stone, quite large, of chalky composition, and it did indeed glow in the dark to an extent far more than its whiteness alone would produce.

Holmes bent over it and struck a vesta to more closely examine its surface. At length, he touched the stone and then sniffed at the tips of his fingers. 'Part of the surface has been treated with phosphorous, Watson, which accounts for the luminosity. It absorbs the light by day and gives it out in darkness.'

I tried to lift the stone but realized that whilst I could do so it was extremely heavy.

I remarked on this to Holmes who nodded and remarked, 'Yet someone has moved it, several times recently.'

He walked over to another of the stones and indicated a depression at its foot.

'You will notice that the earth scar is of such a shape that it almost certainly was caused by the weight of that same stone. See, there are other such scars. It has been recently moved around quite frequently.'

'How can you tell when it was moved?'

'Come, Watson, these scars would be overgrown with grass or otherwise blurred by weather were they not recently made. Why would someone daub a boulder and move it around in a semi-circle? An interesting question, my dear Watson.'

He had been right to use the words 'semi-circle', because further exploration did not reveal any ground scars to indicate that the boulder had rested near the stones on the southern part of the henge. We were about to start our walk back to the White Hart when one other item of interest drew our attention. I first noticed the distant drone of an aircraft engine and found nothing unusual in it, being as we were in a military zone and assumed that the machine was being piloted by a member of the Royal Flying Corps. The plane came from the direction of the sea and flew low over the henge and ourselves in a northerly direction. Then it evidently turned and again flew low; this time back in the direction of the sea.

We waited a few minutes until we were reasonably certain that the aircraft would not return before we started to stroll on the Amesbury road toward our hostelry.

I had said nothing of the incident and neither had Holmes until, about five minutes into our walk, I broke the silence. 'I was surprised that our aircraft returned in the direction from which it had come. I had assumed that it was returning from reconnaissance in France.'

'Watson, you assume then that only our own flying machines are capable of making such flights.'

'You mean that you think it might have been a German aeroplane?'

'I do not merely think that it was, Watson. I know that it was. There is a particular hum that each type of engine makes by which they can be identified. The engine which makes that particular sound originated from the Kline works at Essen. You forget, Watson, that for the past twelve years I have dwelt in Sussex, quite close to an airfield. I have observed the development of aviation with great interest. For quite a while past it has been possible to cross the English Channel in a flying machine, but a return journey without landing to refuel the machine has fortunately been impractical, thus making the Germans rely upon Zeppelins to carry out their air raids. I say fortunately because these vast air balloons are extremely vulnerable to anti-aircraft fire. A wave of aircraft, dropping bombs and able to return to base would be another thing entirely. Even during peacetime the Kline people were working upon an aircraft which could perform such a dreadful deed and return safely. Tonight we have learned that they have indeed succeeded, at least to an extent.'

'What do you mean by "to an extent"?'

'I mean that they now have an aircraft capable of crossing and then recrossing the Channel. But I doubt as yet if they have a machine capable of doing so whilst carrying bombs. What we encountered was doubtless a reconnaissance plane. But we must inform the authorities.'

I found the thought that our observers had missed what we had encountered rather hard to accept. 'Do you think those authorities are unaware of it, Holmes?'

'My dear Watson, I have survived to an age at which nothing surprises me. One could always have been forgiven for imagining that Scotland Yard would have more chance of solving crimes with all their vast resources than a simple soul such as your humble servant.'

I would never have been able to think of Holmes as

either a 'simple soul' or a 'humble servant', but I made no comment, merely taking the point which he made.

At breakfast I discovered that Holmes had changed his mind about several of these details that we had discussed previously. 'I believe we will conceal our findings of last evening, Watson, until we have had a chance to investigate further. Moreover I believe that we will change the plans for us to be taken to the army camp to reside. We will stay here at the inn, at least for a night or two.'

Later that day, the sergeant called for us and took us to the Garrison Theatre which turned out to be a very large hut with a stage fashioned from ammunition boxes at one end. There were curtains which could be drawn across the proscenium made from, it seemed to me, a number of army blankets sewn together. Similar materials draped the back wall of the hut and a much used upright piano was standing to one side of this makeshift stage. There were electric lamps backed by portions of large catering tins, forming a row of footlights, and a homemade spotlight completed the clever theatrical arrangements. We would find these things duplicated at a dozen other venues.

As for the great performance itself, ourselves aside there were two other performers: a couple who presented marionettes. They brought with them what looked for all the world like an overgrown toy theatre. They were middle-aged people, and from their performance they were obviously professionals. The Mini-Follies they called their performance, which seemed apt to describe a series of puppets which performed music hall songs and dances. A miniature Sam Mayo sang 'I'm Only Here for the Day', and there was a can-can dancer as if straight from the Moulin Rouge, and a tiny Hetty King sang and danced her way through "All the Nice Girls Love a Sailor'. The couple stood upon a bench at the rear of their little theatre and operated the puppet strings with wooden cross-pieces attached to them. They also supplied the voices, and the whole thing was splendid, had it not been marred by the musical accompaniment. It had not occurred to me that I would have to play for any other acts that were involved!

In fact for me the whole performance was a nightmare. I managed to play the background for Holmes well enough, and my solo act at the piano went satisfactorily because I encouraged community singing. But the overture and even my rendition of the National Anthem would need to be heard to be believed.

But the soldiers were a good audience, doubtless bored by their isolation on the plain and glad enough to see a few fresh faces and persons not khaki-clad.

After the performance I had a chance to chat with Mr and Mrs Brand who presented the Mini-Follies. In congratulating them upon their performance I managed to stammer a few words of apology for my musical shortcomings. They hastened to assure me that it was unimportant, as they packed away their mannikans into a large suitcase. Mr Brand closed the lid and I saw that it was an expensive affair in cowhide with the name Brand embossed upon the case. Its appearance was marred only by a scuff in the leather near the gold lettering.

Brand caught my eye, I suppose, because he said, 'You see

that mark, it was caused by a tiger's claws when we were with a circus.'

Holmes, who was hovering in the background, joined us to ask, 'How interesting to work in a circus. Did you perform the act which we so much enjoyed tonight?'

'Why yes, but we prefer entertaining the troops!'

Soon it was time for the sergeant to drive us back to the inn. He raised no eyebrow at our desire to stay on there.

'I can't blame you for wanting to remain at the Hart; nice to be able to get a drink whenever you like, eh?'

We chuckled dutifully, but when we were alone Holmes spoke to me in a very serious tone. 'Watson, can you imagine a tiger claw making that scar on Brand's suitcase? It is neatly done, as with a razor, and I imagine it is through the deliberate removal of a letter from their names.'

'You mean there was perhaps an "s" on the end, to say "Brands"?'

'I think not; were the name a plural there would be a "the" preceding it, as in "The Brands". No, I think there was at one time an extra letter to their name, for example, a "t", to make "Brandt".'

'A German name, eh? Come, Holmes, they hardly struck me as being Germans.'

'Why also then did they suggest that they had performed in a circus?'

'Why should they not have?'

'Because, Watson, their act is of such a nature as to be quite unsuitable for that form of entertainment, where all but half of the audience would simply have a view of two people standing on a bench, and just their backs at that!'

'But surely, Holmes, the theatrical world is full of people

who change their names, and the British Isles have a great many people with German names that they have changed. Yet you seem to be suspicious of the Brands. Of what do you suspect them and in what context? Nothing is missing to my knowledge and I have heard of no other recent wrongdoing that they could have been connected with.'

'You say that there has been no wrongdoing, Watson. Cast your mind back to last evening if it is capable of that. You will remember that we saw a phosphorous-treated stone that had been placed near one of the Stonehenge uprights. You will perhaps also remember that we heard the engine of a German aircraft which appeared to fly from the direction of the sea, then turn and fly low over Stonehenge before returning from whence it had come. The pilot had a mission, to see that stone and where it had been placed.'

'You mean the stone which glowed in the dark had been placed to give a message?'

'I thought we had already established that fact, Watson, from finding the scars of its previous settings. The pilot was reading a coded message. Now in looking for the agent who would control the operation from this side of the Channel one would perhaps be excused for suspecting someone of Germanic descent. But it becomes more than idle suspicion when one discovers such a person who has traces of phosphorous on his finger-ends.'

I started, 'What . . . you have perceived such traces?'

'Quite so, Watson, I am not unobservant. I was watching Brand manipulate his mannikins from his high perch as I stood in the wings, if such you can call a draped army blanket. When the lights dimmed for Brand's own miniature spotlight to operate I noticed a glow from his fingertips. It was slight, and I do not imagine he even noticed it himself, especially as his hands were raised above his head to manipulate those cross-pieces which control the strings.'

What my friend had said made good sense, despite the coincidental nature of it all. If we had stumbled upon a nest of enemy espionage on our first day on Salisbury Plain, what enormous luck, especially when our mission was simply to accustom ourselves to the rigours of giving troop concerts!

'To whom shall we communicate this information? To Mycroft directly or to the local commanding officer?'

'At present to neither, Watson. We will simply observe and make absolutely sure of our facts first. In the morning we will set about some means of observing the henge during the hours of daylight, without ourselves being seen. Why do you not take to your bed? I intend to sit here for an hour or two and ponder the matter.'

CHAPTER THREE

The Cat and Mouse Game

'I trust you slept well, my dear Watson?'

There was a hint of sarcasm in my friend's voice as I joined him at the breakfast table. Readers of my past accounts of the exploits of Sherlock Holmes will know that I am apt to sleep rather too well as far as the length of my slumber is concerned. Holmes on the other hand tends to sleep when the opportunity presents itself, which has been often in the past not at all for quite lengthy periods. There were times, back in the halcyon days at Baker Street, when only the gentle puffing of his pipe would betray Holmes's state of sleeping or waking. But this particular morning I observed that Holmes was extremely wakeful, and gave me the impression that he had been in such a condition for several hours.

He gestured towards a bundle in the corner of the parlour. 'During your slumber I have not been idle, my dear fellow. As soon as the landlord appeared at six of the clock I informed him of my intense interest in ornithology.'

'An intense interest which you must have developed

since you went to live in Sussex; for I can remember only a passing interest in birds on your part, and that just when they had some direct bearing upon your work. You are an apiarist rather than an aviary cologist?'

'Watson, an ornithologist is a bird watcher. I intend to watch birds, and other things, from the safety of that hide which I have borrowed from our host. His brother is a keen bird watcher.'

I began to understand what was in his mind. 'I see. You intend to watch in the vicinity of Stonehenge from a hide, to see if anyone moves the phosphorous stone.'

'Of course, and with that in mind I have organized everything we will need, including a lamp and a flask of coffee. Now hasten with your breakfast, Watson, for the game may well be afoot!'

As we made to leave the inn our host offered the use or a dog cart or even two bicycles, but Holmes waved these kind offers aside. 'It will do my friend and I good to walk, for it is only a mile or two. Oh, and landlord, might I beg you not to mention our departure or its intent to anyone else. The "others" may beat us to it!'

The landlord touched his nose. 'Very good, sir, wouldn't want anyone else to spot the bittern before you!'

After we were out of earshot on the lane I shifted my end of the ungainly green canvas-covered bundle from one shoulder to the other, searching for a comfortable way of bearing it and said, 'Holmes, did you tell him that you were seeking to spot a bittern? Why, that species does not occur on Salisbury Plain! I imagine the nearest specimen would be found in the Scottish Highlands.'

'Oh I realize that, Watson, but I had to invent a reason

for my sudden interest where I had expressed none before. I told our host that a poacher had advised me of a sighting of a bittern. Of course, he will be sure that we are not going near Stonehenge, because even if the bittern existed it would hardly appear in such open terrain.'

The nature of the countryside about the henge had occurred to me too, but from the point of view of our own concealment. However, I trusted to my friend's forethought in this matter.

We reached sight of the henge within the hour, having stopped two or three times to rest and change ends of the bundle. But Holmes seemed to think that we were early enough, once he had espied that the phosphorous stone was still in the position where it had been when we had last set eyes upon it.

'But there is no time to be lost, Watson, for it will take us a while to raise this hide and, having done so, to conceal it.'

He was right of course, for it took us quite a while to find a place to raise the hide so that it could be secluded. Eventually I noticed that the side of the lane furthest from the henge had a ditch and a hedge. I suggested that we consider this.

Holmes was pleased with the idea. 'Excellent, Watson. You have, as ever, a good eye. I imagine you were always the first to spot Dervishes, what?'

I breathed hard. 'There were never too many Dervishes in India or Afghanistan, Holmes.'

He grunted with irritability. 'You well know my meaning!'

We raised the canvas on its poles, as low-pitched as was practical and with its spy slits facing the henge. Then we gathered up as many branches and pieces of shrub and scrub as we could muster to conceal our little grotto. Holmes brought forth the field glasses and green rag-decorated headgear which he had borrowed from our landlord. Then we settled in for a long wait, hoping against hope that we would not be discovered by anyone, wrongdoers or otherwise.

We were fortunate in that respect because no one approached from the east, which was our most vulnerable side. A few people and the odd army vehicle passed along the lane without seeing us, but there were very few visitors to Stonehenge itself, which of course would have not been the case in peacetime. Since the war had entered its most harassing aspect most people not in the forces were engaged in some sort of work of national importance.

The time passed with our taking turns to observe with the glasses. I must confess that I did in fact see many interesting birds and an animal or two including rabbits, a badger and quite a few of the silvery grey squirrels, rather bearing out Holmes's prediction concerning Lord Gorse's sin!

Then suddenly at about three of the clock in the afternoon I was about to pour us some coffee when Holmes nudged me and placed a long bony finger to his pursed lips.

He hissed, 'You see, Watson, just to the south of the henge, a figure approaches; a male figure, and it could well be Brand. See — he carries a sack-covered object.'

I was equally quiet in my reply. 'Could be a poacher carrying traps, or a firearm?'

But it soon became clear that it was neither Brand nor yet a poacher, but a 'gentleman of the road' which we soon recognized from the fact that he had rags wrapped about his feet, and his clothing at closer inspection was certainly that of a tramp. Unfortunately for us he chose to seat himself upon a boulder on the northern side of the henge, quite close to the phosphorous stone. He unwrapped the sacking to reveal a stick with a forked end and another with a notch cut near one end. From beneath his voluminous overcoat he produced a tin can with a wire carrying handle. Any boy scouts among my readers will guess the rest, that he improvised a means of cooking with these objects. The notched stick leaned through the forked one, bearing the tin hung by its handle. He built a small fire and was soon cooking whatever noxious mixture reclined within the can. There was nothing we could do save wait for the wanderer to finish cooking and eating, and I feared that he might even follow his repast with forty winks! But suddenly this became less likely with the appearance of a second figure and this indeed proved to be Brand, carrying a toolbag. He was modestly but respectably enough dressed to provide a contrast with the tramp. I imagined that he was no happier to see this gentleman than we had been. He hung around, as if waiting for the tramp to depart, indeed perhaps expecting it. He affected gazing at Stonehenge as if he were a visitor. He took out his watch and studied it, returning it to his waistcoat pocket. He hesitated, then walked up to the seated tramp with an ingratiating smile upon his face. We could see very clearly through our lenses but could not hear what was said, however much we strained our ears.

His hand slid into a pocket and Holmes whispered to me, 'He is going to fall back on bribery.'

Holmes was right, for Brand's hand came forth with a

small collection of silver which he tipped into the tramp's hand so eagerly extended. We were grateful to observe that the tramp packed his traps and hurried off, in the direction of the White Hart.

Brand waited for the tramp to be out of sight and sound and a good five minutes beyond that before he started to show any interest in the stone. Then sure enough he moved over to it and opened his tool bag, taking therefrom an object which appeared to be a very hefty lever. With this he raised the stone, causing it to topple after expending considerable effort. Then he rolled it, mainly with his hands but now and then enlisting the services of the lever to get it over an obstacle. Eventually he managed to line it up with one of the depressions where it had evidently lodged before, and with much pushing, shoving and raising he managed to get the stone standing firm and proud. It was in a position two or three places to the west of the centre pallisade. All the while he was thus engaged he frequently ceased his labours to scan the area for signs of life, but was unhampered by it, little knowing that Holmes and I were watching him like the hawks which we would be expected by an observer to be seeking. Finally he packed his lever away in his tool bag and set off back in the direction from which he had come.

After it was safe to do so we emerged from the hide and made our way over to the stone which had not been differently placed. I appealed to Holmes, 'We must go straight to the commander of the West Cornwall Rifles and tell him exactly what has happened!'

Holmes looked thoughtful and it was several seconds before I got his answer. 'No, Watson, I have another plan!

We will move the stone and see if this has any effect upon the progress of the fighting on the Western Front. Come, jackets off, sleeves rolled, for we have no lever and must improvise.'

It took us a long time to move the stone, most of that time spent in pondering a method. Eventually we used the guy ropes from the hide to topple the stone, with each of us pulling an end. It was not easy but we managed it. Then Holmes devised a method of rolling the stone onto the spread canvas, which we then pulled between us in the direction we desired. Holmes had decided that we would place it on the extreme left of the semi-circle. We managed to replant the stone and then, as we packed everything, we spent quite a while cleaning all traces of phosphorous from our fingers.

'Whatever we do Brand must not suspect what we have done, Watson!'

We made ready to return to the inn, but waited for dusk so that we might tell if the flying machine would again pass and repass Stonehenge. Sure enough, as night fell we heard the drone of its engine and experienced the strange sounds and all but sight of the previous night.

Holmes suddenly brightened. 'Come, Watson, we have work to do still before we return. I believe that the pilot of the plane has been deceived into believing that he has seen what Brand had intended him to. Now if we return the stone to the place where he had moved it to we may, without endangering anything, make him unaware that we have discovered his secret. This would mean that we might be able to get someone in authority to witness that which we have seen, assuming that he repeats the procedure.'

I considered his words carefully; I understood his plan. But a part of me was for getting Brand apprehended at once, lest he should escape from the grasps of authority. However, I aided Holmes in returning the stone to where we had taken it. We were both of us extremely exhausted by the time we got back to the inn and I was all for taking a short nap before preparing for the concert in which we were to participate, but Holmes insisted that we study the map of the Western Front which was in his bedroom. He spread it across his cot and pointed to its semi-circular nature. 'Imagine the northern side of Stonehenge, represented here by a half circle from Arras to Mons. Last night the stone rested in a position very roughly represented therefore by a village called Duvalier. Now, here is this morning's paper, Watson, and I would like you to turn to the first page after the editorial and tell me what the headline is of the principal article.'

Swiftly I turned to the correct page and read, aloud,

ALLIED PUSH AT DUVALIER REPELLED BY HUNS

At midnight an allied push was met by an unexpected force of German infantry and forced to retreat to prepared positions . . .

I trailed off at that point, amazed at what I had read, considering Holmes's words.

At length I spoke. 'Good heavens, it could be coincidence, but it seems unlikely to be.'

Holmes chuckled, 'It is no coincidence, Watson, but we can only prove it by the news that we will read in tomorrow morning's paper. Brand moved the stone to a position very roughly where another village, Villefont, lies. But we moved it to where Aumontpont might be. With luck that is where the Germans will expect activity, and with even more luck might make troop movements which could weaken their position at Villefont. You might feel that we are playing god, Watson, but it is no good making accusations that we cannot substantiate.'

That night I found my role on the pianoforte more difficult; especially as I played merry tunes for Brand and his puppets. Holmes was alert, but careful not to be perceived to be so. A superb actor, he still played the role of a concert violinist doing his bit by entertaining the troops to perfection.

I was early down to breakfast for once, but I still failed to beat Holmes to the table. He was already studying the morning paper when I appeared.

'Good morning, my dear Watson, I trust you slept well; it is a splendid day. I have already been out for a short stroll and the country air has done my nicotine-filled lungs a power of good.'

As ever he was exasperating, irritating in his irony. He was in fact Sherlock Holmes! I did not bother to remonstrate, but merely waited for him to tire of taunting me. Indeed I decided to play him at his own game. 'So you did not wait for the newspapers to be delivered to the inn but walked to the village to buy them at the earliest possible opportunity. You were absolutely right in your deduction that the allied attack at Villefont would be successful.'

He smiled and dropped the sarcasm in his voice, 'Well

done, Watson, you have observed that the newspaper I am reading does not have the words "White Hart" scribbled above its top lines of print, and of course you know me well enough to realize that I would not have taunted you if the news was not good. See for yourself, old fellow, we have scored a hit!'

He passed the paper to me, folded that I might find the article quickly. I only needed to read the headline . . .

ALLIES GAIN GROUND IN PUSH AT VILLEFONT

Holmes attacked his kippers with vigour. 'We have a dilemma now, Watson. We do not know if we are suspected by anyone who does not have the best of intentions towards our country and its cause. I must think of a way that we might speak with the officer in command without drawing special attention. It should be done as soon as possible. Come, we will take the landlord's dog cart to the army camp where we are supposed to appear tonight. Fortunately that is where the HQ is and with luck we can gain an interview without having to tell any underling, which could be dangerous.'

The sentry at the gates of the camp was at first unwilling to admit us, but a sergeant was sent for who examined the papers which we carried, and specified a performance at the very place.

'Very well, gentlemen. I will escort you to our garrison theatre but you are many hours too early; I'm not sure if you will be permitted to remain: you were not expected until eight o'clock. However, come with me and I will show you what you wish to see.'

The huge hut was unlocked and we were shown the stage area as Holmes requested. He walked onto the assembly of ammunition boxes and stamped his foot with petulance. 'Do you really expect me to use such a rostrum? Let me tell you, my colleague and I have played at the Royal Albert Hall and other venues of equal importance! I demand to see your commanding officer!'

I was amazed that the sergeant was impressed by Holmes's words for had I been he I would have had us thrown out! But obviously the soldier had to consider his position in view of such a seemingly important musician.

A veil will be drawn over the red tape that had to be untied before we actually stood before the commanding officer himself. But once we stood there before his desk Holmes relaxed our aliases and revealed our real identities. He had a letter from Mycroft which certainly did the trick. Between us we explained all the details of our bird-watching activities and our manipulation of the espionage that was taking place.

Holmes was all for continuing the subterfuge of moving the stones each evening but Colonel Malt was not. 'As leader of Southern Command I could not possibly allow such events. I can only act upon your information, and question this Brand fellow and try and get to the bottom of it.'

But Holmes would not accept this. 'I will compromise with you, Colonel; why do you not take our bird-watching stance and see what happens for yourself. That way you can catch Brand in the act, so to speak. Then if you will not place the stone to form another false trail you can at least remove it and finish the whole thing. As for Watson and myself, I feel that our work here will finish with tonight's performance. Tomorrow, once I am sure that Brand has been apprehended, we will return to London to be assigned to our continental expedition.'

The colonel set the ruse into action and that very evening he and an armed solider watched from a hide, and when they had observed Brand's activities for themselves they arrested him under a section of the Defence of the Realm Act, and confiscated the stone which was collected in an army vehicle.

Later we conferred again with the colonel, and of course the elderly soldier was full of praise for our work. 'We had thought it safer that the very heart of British strategy should be carried out away from the front line, but of course your timely intervention has shown flaws in that system. However, all appears safe now.'

Holmes's eyes narrowed at this statement. 'Not quite, Colonel. You see, you appear to be overlooking the most important aspect of all.'

Malt bristled like an elderly hedgehog. 'Something I have overlooked? What?'

'Something extremely important: the question is where and how did Brand obtain information that should not have been known to anyone outside of that inner sanctum where the war strategy is planned. Is it well enough concealed?'

'Why certainly; only those whose loyalty to their country and the army are ever allowed access to that which passes as the HQ of Southern Command, but which as you know is possibly the most vital and secret place in the whole country.'

Holmes nodded and smiled kindly, but his words were spoken sternly. 'The best laid plans of mice and men, eh Colonel? How many people have any sort of access to the most sensitive information?'

'Four of us only, Holmes. Myself, my adjutant Captain James, a soldier almost as experienced and senior as myself, and our secretary, Lieutenant Hopkins, a Sandhurst man, beyond any sort of doubt as to loyalty and ability to keep secrets.'

I chimed in at this point. 'That is three, Colonel. You mentioned four?'

'Quite right, Watson. The fourth member of the team is a splendid fellow who is trustworthy enough to be our runner. He takes highly secret documents to other branches of HQ, where there are no field telephone lines, or where it would be unwise to use them, by means of a motorcycle.'

Holmes asked, 'His name, Colonel?'

'Sergeant Johnson. Splendid fellow, officer material really, but too useful at the moment as he is, what?'

The colonel chuckled at his own words and continued an obviously lifetime's work of training his waxed moustache.

Holmes looked thoughtful. 'Johnson. It's a common enough name. For example, there is a Sergeant Johnson who operated the spotlight at our performance at the garrison theatre.'

The colonel brightened, 'The same fellow. Excellent chap, understands electricity thoroughly, as well as morse code and all those sort of things.'

Sherlock Holmes looked extremely thoughtful indeed and he exchanged a glance with me before he spoke. 'Does he work the lights at all of Brand's performances in the area?'

'Why, yes. Most of them anyway.'

'Has he appeared to have any other contact with Brand?'

'None whatever that I am aware of.'

The colonel could not guess the drift that the mind of Sherlock Holmes was taking; but through years of association I began to think that I could, especially when these words were combined with those which followed. 'Is he aware of the apprehension of Brand, or was it kept as secret as I had wished?'

'He should not be; Mrs Brand was also apprehended, and the pair of them taken to London by road.'

'Where are his properties at this moment; his marionette set-up, for instance?'

'They were taken to the theatre. To the best of my knowledge they are still there.'

'Then please be sure that they remain where they are, and also be sure that Johnson is not informed concerning recent events.'

Soon it was time for us to make our way to a garrison theatre, though not the one at which we had appeared before. This one was a little further out upon the Plain, and when we arrived there Holmes checked to see if Brand's equipment was there, which indeed it was, standing in its cases in the wings. The cases were locked, but Holmes was able to open them very easily with a short length of wire. I thought I knew that which was in his mind. He intended to give some sort of performance with Brand's puppets.

'When Brand is announced, as I will arrange for him to be, the audience will see puppets, but of course not the operator. I hope that Johnson, from his position with the spotlight at the opposite end of the hall especially will be unaware of the change. I will perform a very limited selection from Brand's repertoire. My vocal prowess will only permit one song that is within my range. But I am more interested in the puppet which performs a dance, the skeleton you know.'

'You mean the one where the spotlight contributes to that dislocating effect?'

'Yes, my dear Watson, that is exactly what I mean.'

We got through our own parts of the performance well enough, and then it was time for me to rise from the piano and announce, 'Gentlemen, the next act. "The Brands" will be performed in a slightly curtailed form due to the indisposition of Mrs Brand. However, I feel sure that the remaining member of the act will give us a very amusing and amazing performance. Gentlemen, I give you the Brand Marionettes!'

It was with some trepidation that I returned to the piano and played the fanfare to introduce the act. The tiny theatre stood there as usual with only a shadowy figure on a raised bench visible with the light concentrated on the miniature stage. First, the Hetty King puppet entered, and what was lacking in vocalism was made up for as the figure was manipulated in an almost professional manner by Holmes, as he croaked the words of 'All the Nice Girls Love a Sailor'. There was applause at the end of the song, though less than there would have been for Brand. But then the skeleton figure appeared and, to the blinking of the spotlight, performed its strange antics. I was relieved when Holmes's presentation of the puppeteer came to an end.

Gratefully I tinkled out 'God Save the King' and then the audience started to wander out of the hut. Holmes did not even bother to repack Brand's properties as he emerged from behind the curtain. 'Follow me, Watson, and show no astonishment at what I might say or do.'

I followed his example as he strode over to where Johnson was dismantling the spotlamp. I noticed that it had a shutter mechanism which he had used for the lighting effects for the skeleton. He was packing this carefully away.

Holmes casually spoke to him. 'Sergeant Johnson, we have to go to Colonel Malt's HQ to discuss with him arrangements for the future. Our regular driver seems to have departed; do you think you could take us there?'

The sergeant seemed quite happy to drive us there in an army vehicle which turned out to be a motorcycle with a fitted sidecar.

'Hope you don't mind a bumpy ride, gents. I'll get you there safely, have no fear.'

A bumpy ride it proved to be, but Holmes was full of lighthearted banter the whole way. I followed his lead and felt sure that he could not possibly suspect that Holmes's plans included himself. (Which by this time I felt sure that they did!) Our progress and entrance into HQ was actually simpler through Johnson's presence than might otherwise have been the case. Indeed Johnson played into Holmes's hands as he insisted on accompanying us to the colonel's office. His confidence made me wonder if Holmes could be mistaken in his suspicions concerning the sergeant's involvement in espionage.

The colonel, fully in our confidence, played his role quite

well, considering his background. 'Well, gentlemen, another successful performance I trust, what?'

Holmes went straight for the point, so to speak. 'Thank you, yes Colonel, though the puppets were a bit below standard. Take the dancing skeleton, for instance. It did not react to your morse code quite as you might have expected Johnson, because I had been pressed into service.'

The sergeant started, 'What, you were the puppeteer, Mr Hailsham?'

'The name is Sherlock Holmes. My colleague is none other than my Boswell, Dr John Watson.'

All blood seemed to have departed from Johnson's face, but he was still full of protests just in case, I imagined, the whole episode was some kind of joke.

'Oh, very funny. Rehearsing a new act are we, gentlemen?'

'Not as thoroughly as you have rehearsed your morse code, Sergeant. I, of course, can read that cypher and have that rare ability required on this occasion to continue manipulating a puppet whilst so doing.'

'Is this some sort of accusation . . . ?'

'It is more, it is a statement of fact. Whilst I manipulated the strings you flashed to me in morse the name of a French village, Vachen.'

It was the colonel's turn to start, and the monocle fell from his left eye. 'By George, that is the name of the area where a fresh advance is planned for two nights from now! You know that, Johnson, and you were not aware that Brand was not on the stage. According to Holmes, you flashed the name of that town to him, doubtless believing that Brand would convey that information in the fullness of time by means of a luminous boulder, arranged so that it could be seen clearly by a German airman and conveyed by him to their high command. This would have meant that our attempted advance would have been expected with disastrous consequences. You, sir, are a traitor to your country, and a firing squad will make sure that you never betray your country again.'

At this point the colonel made to touch a bell push on his desk, but Johnson stopped him by suddenly producing a long, pointed dagger from beneath his tunic. He held it to the colonel's throat and turned his face toward us.

No doubt he was about to blackmail us into inactivity by the threat of driving the blade into the colonel's throat, but almost instantly there was an explosion, a flash, and the dagger fell from Johnson's now profusely bleeding hand.

Dear reader, I am as you know an old soldier and as such I would hardly have dabbled in such muddy waters, as the past few days had produced, without my service revolver. There was time for only one shot and I took a great chance in firing it at all. But the element of surprise was on my side. That his hand was hit was largely luck; that he was hit at all a little fortunate I admit. I followed my advantage by levelling the revolver steadily, pointing it at his body.

I found myself taking command. 'The game is up, Johnson. Raise your hands above your head. Colonel, pray touch your electric bell; useful what? We didn't have those in my day.'

When Johnson had been marched away with a steely grip on each arm by two big soldiers, the colonel breathed again as he congratulated me on my quick action. 'My dear fellow, what can I say? I possibly owe you my life! Once a soldier always a soldier, what?'

I stuttered something which I thought represented honest modesty but I admit there was a shake in my voice. As one frequently does after such a shock I turned upon Holmes, the only person I could think of to blame for having been exposed to the situation at all.

But my friend soon mollified me, as ever. 'My dear Watson, from long experience I knew that you were a man to be relied upon in a tight corner. Moreover I knew that you would not have set forth this day without your service revolver!'

Later we would learn that Brand had been hanged, rather like one of his own marionettes, as a traitor. Had he not been a citizen of His Majesty (although of German descent) he would doubtless have been offered the alternative of a firing squad.

We partook of a late meal of cold beef and mashed potatoes at the White Hart where our jovial host remarked, as he served us, 'Well gents, you must have been a big success with the army this evening?'

Sherlock Holmes smiled ironically and said, 'Yes, landlord, I rather think we were!'

CHAPTER FOUR

Holmes and the Entente Cordiale

Back in wartime London our first port of call was the Diogenes Club to give Mycroft our version of the events which we knew would already be known to him. I suppose I had half expected praise, at least for Holmes, concerning our exploits. But as ever, Mycroft was Mycroft!

Sherlock's plump brother sat down in his armchair, attempted to cross one elegantly trousered leg over the other, then seemingly he gave up as if the effort was too much for him.

Instead he blew some cigar smoke into the air and addressed us with a voice that was touched with irritability. 'Sherlock, Watson, you go to Salisbury Plain on my behalf and discover a vipers' nest which you seemingly burnt out. But then you proceed to lose the principal of this trio of spies that you had so cleverly discovered.'

I asked, 'Brand has escaped?'

'No, he is in custody at the Tower; he will hang.'

Sherlock seemed to catch Mycroft's meaning very swiftly. 'You mean that Brand was not the brains of the trio? It certainly was not Sergeant Johnson, so it had to be Brand's partner, the woman who assisted him with his puppets. You are going to tell me that in real life it was she who pulled the strings? Well, you surprise me, for I could not be absolutely certain that she was even involved. No matter, she is safely in custody, is she not?'

'She most certainly is not!'

Holmes and I were both taken aback and waited for Mycroft to enlarge on what he had said.

'Being a woman, her guards were lax. Like you, they possibly even believed that she had no great involvement with espionage. But Brand, under questioning, has admitted that he took his orders from her. As I say, the guards were lax and did not place her in any form of restraint upon the journey to London. A stop was made with the vehicle near Haywards Heath, where the terrain is particularly densely wooded. The vehicle could not follow her and the men, on foot were too slow and clumsy. They lost the scent, Sherlock, and I hold you responsible.'

Sherlock Holmes's voice was tinged with sarcasm. 'Does this mean that I will be shot at dawn?'

I tried to break the tension with an age-old army joke, 'At least you can't have me shot at dawn because I never rise before nine of the clock . . . your brother will tell you that!'

But Mycroft shook his great head with severity. 'It is no laughing matter. Sherlock, you must find her before she manages to give us the slip entirely. If she makes contact with the enemy, heaven knows what secrets she has discovered to pass on to them!'

My friend Sherlock Holmes shook all irony aside, leaned forward in his chair and averred, 'I will devote all my energies to apprehending this woman, Mycroft. Please give me all possible details that you might have learned from Brand and Johnson. After all, we are not even entirely certain as to her real name.'

Mycroft spoke ruefully, 'Neither are we, the secret service or I, for she evidently has used many aliases and is a woman of many parts. However, here is a document which I had the foresight to prepare, knowing that you would be happy to try to make good your mistakes.'

We left the Diogenes Club with a general feeling of gloom. After all, we both had felt that we had performed a great service for our country. Indeed, I still think I can say that we had, for we had discovered the source of that leak which had bedevilled our forces on the Western Front. Moreover, we were responsible in leading to the capture of a trio of presently and potentially dangerous enemy agents; hardly was it our fault that the guards had slipped up. Indeed, I believe to this day that Mycroft felt the same; he merely placed this blame upon his brilliant brother that he might goad him into performing the seemingly impossible.

Holmes started slowly to recover his spirits as we strolled along Pall Mall. 'Watson, what is the first thing one should do in a situation like ours?'

After a moment or two of thought I replied, 'Calm down and have a cup of tea?'

Holmes chuckled. 'The cup that cheers nor yet inebriates, eh? Exactly what I had expected you to say, Watson, for you are to be trusted for your sanity in a maniacal universe. Come, here is a likely place, near enough to Trafalgar Square to cater for the few tourists that are about in these depressing times.'

He led me into a café where there were marble-topped tables and waitresses in black silk with neat white caps and pinafores. A place that had kept its standards even in wartime. We ordered a pot of tea for two and a selection of pastries which proved to be rather home-made looking, with carrot in place of cherry and a complete lack of icing or cream. However, the tea was hot, strong and up to standard.

Holmes poured the tea, and then unfurled the paper document that Mycroft had handed to him. 'Great Scott, Watson, did I say that Brand's companion might have an alias or two? Well, there are only just short of a dozen here. It seems that friend Brand has well and truly spilled the beans. Names aside there are three different nationalities listed for her: French, German and Hungarian. She has posed as a nurse on the Western Front, a Parisian music hall entertainer, a typewriter operator at the German Embassy in Paris: that would have been in peacetime of course. She is evidently an expert in codes and cyphers and at one time was an agent for the American Pinkerton detective agency. A double-agent when it suits her purpose; a dangerous woman, Watson, especially as we have got only the smallest glimpses of her features. However, as soon as we have finished our tea we will repair to your home, then on to the Charing Cross Hotel, from where we will be able to make our way towards our first port of call.'

'Which is?'

'Haywards Heath, where the scent was lost. Let us see if we cannot pick it up afresh.'

We took a taxi cab to my home where I warned my domestics that I would be away, possibly for a week or two.

My medical work consisted in the main of acting as locum for other doctors. But this was a purely freelance occupation and I was fortunately as free as a bird. I left a fairly substantial sum with the cook, whom I knew could be trusted to settle bills and so forth. Then I packed a few essentials into a carpet bag and went with Holmes to the Charing Cross Hotel where he packed his traps. I wondered why he had not arranged to go straight there that I might join him.

He read my mind as usual, saying, 'Watson, my mind works well whilst I am in a moving vehicle. My brain has not been idle during our trivial converse in the cab.'

I was not so sure that I liked my part of the converse being referred to as trivial, but said nothing. Holmes had decided by now that we would take the train to Haywards Heath from Victoria. Evidently in the folio which Mycroft had handed him there was a sketch map of the exact spot where the guards had left our quarry. We managed to find a first-class smoker despite the extremely curtailed length of the train.

'Holmes, I know we are going to a spot in the woods near Haywards Heath where the scent was lost, but surely by now the trail will be cold. The lady could be anywhere by now. By the way, which of her names should we call her in converse?'

'We will refer to her as Ilona; Ilona Valesca in fact, but Ilona will do. As to your question, I have found by experience that there are few trails that are completely cold to the experienced investigator.'

'I have no doubt that Scotland Yard have been thorough, as well as the secret service people.'

Holmes breathed heavily at these words of mine and said, 'Regarding that, Watson, we shall see.'

We left the train at Haywards Heath station and took a horse-drawn cab, the first I had seen in a year or so, to the place on the Burgess Hill road from where Holmes's sketch map told him we should start. There were signs upon the roadside turf of the frantic activity which must have occurred when Ilona had slipped her leash so to speak. Then we saw the trail of her footprints, her high-heeled boots making this easy to follow for a while. Then, quite suddenly, as the undergrowth and boles of the trees thickened, the trail disappeared. Doubtless as many had done before us, we took first one route, then another, to try to pick up the trail again. I was not as pessimistic as one might suppose concerning Holmes's ability to pick up a trail where none seemed to exist, for I had seen him do it before.

'Watson, what would you do if you were trying to elude pursuers and were experienced enough to know that your distinctive footwear was bound to indicate the route that you were taking?'

'Why I think I might abandon the footwear and carry on in my stockinged feet!'

'Exactly, Watson, and I feel sure that is what Ilona did. Rather than searching for a trail we should now be looking for a discarded pair of high-heeled women's boots, size six, for she has large feet. Here is the final print: now if we look among the bracken we might find the boots.'

We did as he suggested, and find them we did, or rather one of them, and Holmes decided that it would be pointless to seek the other one, having proved his theory. He decided now that the investigation made it sensible to dismiss the cab, and we gave instructions to the cabby to take our luggage to a hostelry which he could recommend. He suggested the Golden Lion, so we knew that our luggage would await us there. Moreover, Holmes told him to book accommodation for us both for the night. I dared to suggest that he should instruct the driver to return for us, to take us to the inn.

But Holmes shook his head. 'No, Watson, for who knows where we will have arrived at by sunset?'

I heard these words and watched the retreating cab with trepidation, but knew in my heart that my friend was wise in his words. Even so, I glanced at the damp undergrowth and did not relish what lay ahead.

But Holmes was optimistic and hearty, 'Come, Watson, we are both stoutly shod and you have your service revolver.'

He spoke with mockery in his voice, doubtless prompted by my recent use of that weapon which did indeed repose inside my jacket, for by now I had experienced enough to know that we were dealing with very dangerous people.

'See, here is a possible trail, Watson. The depressions in the grass made by stockinged feet, ignored by those who were seeking the prints of women's boots.'

I supposed that these depressions could be interpreted as Holmes chose to. We followed the trail, but eventually the tress became so dense that the actual act of any progress became difficult. I guessed that those who had been before us had taken a different trail, be it false or no. Then, worse still, we came upon a sheer brick wall, perhaps some fifteen feet high.

I enquired of my friend, 'Do you think she turned left or right?'

Holmes decided to pause and fill his pipe, which he then ignited with a vesta before he replied, 'Perhaps neither, Watson. Her pursuers might not have expected her to scale this wall.'

'Neither would I! It is beyond my capabilities, and I am an old soldier. Certainly a woman would not attempt it.'

'What if she were to climb a tree and clamber onto the wall in that manner?'

'She might have tried, I suppose, but it would not have been easy. This is obviously the wall of an institution so it will not be simple to negotiate.'

Holmes nodded, but questioned my words. 'It is indeed an institution: it is marked upon my sketch map. It is intended to house those who are considered to be insane; in fact, an asylum. This high wall is intended to retain the inmates and prevent them from breaking out. But the outside is a different matter. Few persons, my dear Watson, attempt to break into an asylum for the insane . . . unless they are candidates for such accommodation.'

His point was a good one.

'So you think it could have been possible for Ilona to scale the wall by climbing a tree?'

'With some difficulty. Just how much we are about to find out. Come, Watson, gird your loins and we will see what can be done.'

Climbing onto the wall by means of one of the trees was hazardous but not too difficult. Holmes managed it more easily than I did, but game leg or no I also achieved it.

From the top of the wall we surveyed what lay inside its

enclosure. Within some hundred yards there stood a large depressing-looking grey stone building with barred windows. Below us there was an expanse of greensward without any sort of ledge to assist in our clambering down. It was clear that escape from the inside would be impossible without a ladder. However, we managed to reach the ground by hanging by our fingertips. This made the drop no more than eight or nine feet and, with the expected impact, we both managed it well for men in middle years!

'Well, Watson, having proved that it is possible to do what we suspect that Ilona did we will make our way to the entrance.'

A terrifying thought occurred to me. 'Holmes, you don't suppose we might be mistaken for lunatics and incarcerated in this dreary-looking place?'

Holmes laughed. 'Oh, Watson, what an ironic stroke of fate that might be. But no, to be serious I believe we can both prove our identity. Mind you, I cannot help but think that we are candidates for such a restraining influence!'

There is perhaps nothing quite so depressing in this world as an institution for the incarceration of the insane. A prison, yes, that too is sombre and harrowing; but the people within the cells (with a very few notable exceptions) deserve the treatment meted out to them. As a medical man I know that the lunatic, so called because he is supposed to be controlled by the movements of the moon, is not a wrongdoer in the ordinary sense and does not deserve to be treated as such. I had visited such places in my professional capacity and was therefore hoping, I suppose, that we would not need to as part of our present occupation.

Fortunately I did not have to conceal these feelings from Holmes because I knew that our views upon the matter were in accord. Nevertheless, my heart sank as we walked round to the front of the building. It was just a huge stone edifice, rather like a hospital save for its barred windows, yet there was this aura of doom as we entered the guarded front doors.

We were accosted by a uniformed doorman who demanded to know our business.

'My name is Watson, Dr John Watson, and this gentleman . . .'

'Oh I see, bringing us a patient are you, Doctor?'

Before I could deny this Holmes spoke. 'My name is Sherlock Holmes and . . .'

Before he could finish his introduction the doorman, with a sympathetic air, said, 'Never mind, they'll soon help you here. Sherlock Holmes, eh? That's a new one, though we do have quite a few Napoleons and a Queen Victoria or two . . .'

I decided to take control of the situation. 'So you have female patients as well as men? Tell me, was there any sort of incident with any of them yesterday?'

He brightened. 'Funny you should ask me that, Doctor, for we did have a rather strange affair concerning someone who we took at first to be one of our ladies. She came round the side of the building, as you did, looking as if she'd been through a hedge backwards. But more unusual still, she had no boots on, and her feet were quite torn and cut up like she had been walking on brambles. She was limping a bit and I grabbed hold of her and took her inside to check if any of our ladies had managed to escape through a window or the like. But a check was made and no one was unaccounted for. She claimed that she had come to visit a friend, a Mary Simpson, but there was no record of her either. So we directed her to the visitors' vehicle which was standing, just about to leave. There's one standing over there now, but I expect you came here in it? Well, well, let's get "Mr Sherlock Holmes" inside!'

As the fellow made to lay hands upon my friend I choked back a chuckle. But Holmes obviously felt that the joke had been taken far enough.

He assumed his most intimidating air. 'Unhand me, there's a good fellow! I am indeed Sherlock Holmes and I am investigating the disappearance of the young woman whom you have described. See, here is my card, and my friend and colleague, Dr Watson, will confirm my identity.'

The doorman began to suspect that he had indeed made a mistake. 'Oh, *that* Dr Watson. Of course, I'm sorry, gents.'

I felt rather sorry for the poor fellow who had made a rather natural mistake.

'I expect you get a lot of customers who believe themselves to be celebrated. Think no more of it.'

But Holmes was impatient now and started to question and doorman. 'Anything you can tell me concerning her appearance and general deportment would be helpful. For instance, did she speak with a local accent?'

'No, sir. I would have said that she was a Scots lady; though I'm no expert upon such matters.'

As we walked over to the vehicle which we were assured would take us into Haywards Heath itself, Holmes remarked, 'A woman of many parts as we already knew; but experienced with British dialects too. Perhaps the driver of this strange vehicle will be able to help us further.'

Perhaps at this point I should describe the vehicle itself. Older readers, or should I say those of my own age, will remember vividly the old horse-drawn charabanc which slowly disappeared soon after the turn of the century. Well, this vehicle looked for all the world like one of those, save that it had a motor engine and driver's seat, complete with steering wheel at the front.

I remarked upon this to Holmes, but as usual he had the answer. 'The same factory that built horse-drawn vehicles for centuries made this very early motor vehicle. Naturally they used a great many existing fitments. It does indeed look like a motorized horse bus! However, the driver may be able to help with our investigations.'

It was fortunate that the driver was indeed the same that had driven the 'strange lady' along with other passengers, to Haywards Heath on the previous day. 'Thought at first that she was one of their loonies, guv'nor, standing there without no boots and looking dishevelled, to say the least. But I took her to Haywards Heath with the others.'

'You took her the whole way to Haywards Heath?'

'Why yes. I do stop a few times on the way for those who live locally, but she went the whole way.'

'Did you happen to notice the direction she took when she left your vehicle?'

'No, I didn't. I was too busy with my engine having overheated, sir. Give me horses any day!'

It was but a few short miles to Haywards Heath, but we spent what little time we had in the rather badly sprung vehicle to discuss what we had learned, little though it was.

'I fail to see, Holmes, how we can pick up the trail at

Haywards Heath, for it will surely have gone cold by now. After all, we do not even know which way she went when she alighted.'

Holmes waxed ironic, 'You fail to see, as you put it. Watson, if you had discarded your boots in emergency; which is what she did, having not the time to think of tying their laces and hanging them round her neck, where would you make for as soon as you arrived at a shopping district?'

'A boot shop?'

Holmes applauded my words, sarcastically. 'Exactly, Watson, the trail may not be as cold as you believed it to be. If she did not quickly obtain a pair of boots her appearance will be remembered locally, I'll wager.'

The driver braked noisily. 'Haywards Heath, centre of town, far as we go!'

We descended gratefully from the rickety omnibus. Holmes glanced sharply around him. There was nothing unusual to see. It was a neat, clean-looking little town with buildings ancient and modern. One of the latter happened to be the shop of a bootmaker and seller, and with one accord we made for that establishment. It proved to be one of those small businesses where the owner plies his trade. The bootmaker sat at his last in the background and the front of the shop was filled with piles of the results of his labours. There were also more cheaply marked boots, evidently the results of intensive labour. It would not have taken an expert in footwear to tell the hand-made from the factory products.

Holmes smiled ingratiatingly at the bootmaker. He had glanced at the name over the shopfront which I had neglected to do. 'Mr Castle, I presume?'

'Yes, sir, the very same. What can I do for you?'

'My name is Sherlock Holmes and this is my friend and colleague Dr Watson. I wonder if I might ask you a few questions?'

The bootmaker sighed wearily. 'There, and I was thinking I might have a couple of customers, or one at least. For you'd be surprised at how many people bring a friend with them when they buy a pair of boots. Well, what are these questions you want to ask me?'

'Mainly I wanted to ask if yesterday yielded any customers that might be described as unusual?'

Castle put down his large curved needle and scratched his thatch of grey hair. 'Let me see now. There was a fellow who wanted me to make him a single boot.'

Holmes nodded wisely. 'I noticed the small circular marks that the ferrule of his wooden leg made in the dust near your door. Evidently he made his enquiry without moving any nearer to you. There are no further signs yet the dust is evenly distributed.'

'He expected me to charge him for one boot! The foot he did have was distorted so I would have needed to spend as much time on it as to make a normal pair. Honestly, what some people expect, Mr Holmes!'

'Quite. For example, the man with the club foot must be a challenge to your skills.'

'How did you know about him? He didn't come in yesterday, not for weeks in fact. I must get the boy to sweep up the dust.'

Holmes had surprised me a little too. But the answer was rather typical of him. 'Come, Mr Castle, there is not a bootmaker as well established as yourself who has not suffered the customer with the club foot. Oh yes, and before you ask me how I know that you are long established, the sign writing over the shop, bearing your name, has not been repainted for at least twelve years, and I have observed your skill with a needle.'

The bootmaker was losing patience and I felt that it was up to me to restore the atmosphere to one of equanimity. I picked up a boot and asked if I could try it on. His manner changed at once as he smelled a possible sale. He seated me and plied his skill with a shoe horn, placing several boots upon my foot until he was satisfied. I paid him the sovereign which he was asking for the boots and considered them a bargain. You could not tell them from a pair made in St James's Street, where they would have cost at least double what I paid.

As he wrapped my purchase he said, 'These will serve you well, Doctor. Mr Holmes, there was another customer yesterday, a little bit unusual. There was a woman, neatly dressed but looking as if she had fallen into a hay cart. She was well spoken, but what really was unusual was the fact that she was wearing only stockings on her feet. She said that she had broken the heel of one of her boots and discarded them both in a fit of pique. I sold her a cheap pair of boots for five bob; she didn't want to invest in better ones.'

I felt quite excited that Holmes had proved right that Ilona had stopped in Castle's boot shop.

I tried to be helpful. 'Could you show Mr Holmes a pair like those she bought?'

He shook his head. 'That I could not for they were the only pair I had as lowly priced. She was more interested in cheapness than quality or even fit; for they were rather on the small side for her.'

Holmes enquired, 'Can you tell us the direction she might have taken when she left?'

'Why yes, sir, as it happens, I can, for she wanted to get to a railway station, or rather a halt, just south of here. Said she could not afford a cab so I told her that Daft Jimmy would take her in his cart for a few pence. He's an unfortunate, sir, nice lad but a bit simple. She went off in his cart in the direction of the railway halt.'

I could not believe in our good fortune but Holmes seemed to be taking it very calmly. 'Could you get this boy Jimmy to take us to the halt in his cart?'

'Why yes, sir, should be easy; he's always hanging around near here. Watch the shop, I'll see what I can do.'

Mr Castle, mellowed by my purchase, went off to seek the unfortunate youth with the cart.

'Daft Jimmy' turned out to be, as northerners would put it, a 'gormless youth', tall, red haired, with an aged army greatcoat and boots that had seen very much better days. There were straws in his hair giving him rather the appearance of the classic village idiot, but I estimated that he was far from idiotic, just a trifle slow on the uptake. His horse and cart, both aged, looked as if they might have been another's cast-offs to match his overcoat.

Holmes treated him with that charm which he always seems to save for unfortunates. 'Mr Castle seems to think that you might take us to the railway halt, where you took the strange lady yesterday. This being so we will pay you for your time and use of your vehicle. Further we would like to ask you a few questions.'

Jimmy looked a bit doubtful at this, saying, 'Well, sir, that will be all right if the questions ain't about figuring, and histrinometry and that. They had to burn down the school to get me out of the mixed infants; and then I were twelve, I think!'

We assured him that our questions would not be connected with education, and he brightened.

He remembered taking the strange lady to the railway halt. 'Oh yes, sir, she only give me tuppence but I din't mind because I was going that way anyway. She had new boots on, so I expect she had spent all her money.'

Holmes asked his questions with clarity but no patronism. 'Did she give any idea where she was making for, Jimmy?'

'She never said, but as she wanted this side of the rails she could only go south; and if she went south she could only go to Brighton 'cause the other trains don't stop here.'

Slow he may have been considered, but he was also logical. When we got to the halt I decided to test his intellect a bit further.

I took a shilling and a penny from my pocket and placed them side by side on my palm and asked, 'Which of these coins would you like to take to pay for our ride in your cart, Jimmy?'

He scratched his head and then said, 'Well, gaffer, my first thought is to take the biggest coin, but then again when I was a nipper me mum always told me that when the cakes was handed round it would be only polite to take the smallest; so I think I'll take that little silver 'un!'

I gravely handed him the shilling, and Holmes and I managed to hold back our laughter until the sounds made by the aged horse's hooves could no longer be heard. Then we collapsed at the side of the railway lines.

Holmes was the first to recover. 'Oh, Watson, I seldom laugh, as you know, but who could resist laughing at that demonstration of craftiness on the part of the unfortunate youth. When the gods see fit to dim the wisdom they sometimes leave a certain artfulness in exchange.'

When we had recovered from our hilarity we started to discuss our plans for the immediate future.

'Holmes, if the train that stops here will only go to Burgess Hill do you intend us to go there and try to pick up her trail again?'

My friend charged his pipe and lit it before he replied. 'There is nothing else we can do, Watson. I am afraid it will be some time before we take up residence at the Golden Lion, or even claim our luggage! I will wire the landlord at the earliest opportunity to hold them. Come, relax old fellow, we have a while to wait for the train.'

'You have a south coast railway timetable?'

'No, but my judgement tells me that we will be waiting for the same train which took Ilona to Burgess Hill yesterday.'

Several Brighton-bound trains thundered past us before the slow-moving train bound for Burgess Hill appeared and shuddered to a stop. It was too small a train for us to seek a first-class smoker so we climbed into the first smoking carriage we could find. As it was, we only just made it safely onto the train for it seemed that no sooner had it ground to a halt than it started tentatively forward again. We had no tickets of course, but I imagined that we would be able to pay for them at Burgess Hill.

We were not the only occupants of the carriage, for a middle-aged lady was already seated therein as we entered the apartment. We sat at the window seats, opposite each other, and I raised my hat to the lady and asked if she had objection to our smoking.

She raised none and fortunately for us turned out to be quite loquacious. 'I don't mind tobacco smoke. I take this train every afternoon, and most of the smokers find their way into it. Mind you, it is unusual for anyone to get on at the halt; wouldn't be surprised if they don't do away with it before long. Mind you, there was a woman who got on there yesterday, got into this carriage, very strange she was. She had on a pair of new boots that seemed to be crippling her. A size too small, if you ask me; some women will do anything to try and make their feet look smaller, won't they? Cheap-looking boots they were too. Mind, her other clothes were quite good quality, though she did look as if she had rolled in a hayfield!'

Sherlock Holmes obviously found it hard to believe his good fortune at being told so much of value without having asked a single question. But he could not resist speeding up the process by asking, 'Did this strange woman descend from the train at the end of the line, at Burgess Hill? I imagine she must have, for I am not aware of any other halts.'

Her answer was a gift, so to speak. 'I was just getting to that. The train slowed down just before we got to the end of the run and, for a few seconds, it stopped just short of Burgess Hill station. Only a few seconds I say, but long enough for her to open the door and drop onto the line. I was flabbergasted! She could have got herself badly hurt. Hardly worth it to save a few pennies was it?'

We grunted our agreements and Holmes looked thoughtful as the train began to slow down. He threw down the sash window and leaned out. 'Quick, Watson, the train is about to stop. Let us emulate our quarry and see what she would have found.'

As the train momentarily stopped we dropped onto the line, having first touched our hats to the middle-aged lady who gasped and said, 'Well, I never. Two more at it. What's the attraction, I wonder?'

I admit that I was almost as surprised myself, and as the train left us there we glanced around us for clues as to where Ilona might have gone next. But our reverie was interrupted by a uniformed official with a large dog of the Alastian variety on a leash. 'Hey, you two, what do you think you are doing on the line?'

Rather to my surprise Holmes took the fellow into his confidence. At least to the extent by identifying himself and suggesting that we were on official government business. The railway official told us that he would need to take us to the station master's office, and to this we raised no objection.

The station master was polite, if a trifle officious, as we stood before him in his small hut of an office.

He said, 'I do not disbelieve your credentials, gentleman, but you can appreciate my position. Passengers are not allowed to alight from the trains except at designated places. Why only yesterday we had a woman who jumped down off the same train as you did. She had no official position to plead either; just a story about looking for a dog that had jumped off the train. She had no ticket, and I was forced to send for the police. Of course I feel sure I need not do so in your case, but . . .'

Holmes interrupted him. 'I wish you would. I need to talk with the local police.'

Then, sir, I suggest you visit the police station which is only a step from here.'

The sergeant at the police station was quite helpful to us. He told us all that he could about the strange woman who had been arrested on the day before. 'She was what we refer to as a "distressed gentlewoman", Mr Holmes. She was very well spoken and told us that she was a Mary Harkness, and gave us an address in Reading. Evidently she had been robbed by some footpads, and her appearance bore this out, for although well dressed her clothes were full of thorns and grasses. They had taken her handbag and even her expensive boots. The brand new cheap ones that she was wearing bore out the story. She had run out of money and wished to proceed to Steyning where some friends were expecting her. We loaned her half a sovereign from the funds we have for the purpose. I have no doubt at all that she will send us a postal order within a few days.'

Alas, I wished I could share this touching faith expressed by this honest policeman.

I wondered if Holmes would put all our cards upon the table, but he did not. 'Sergeant, it is vital that I contact this young woman, concerning the death of a relative, a possible inheritance in fact. Any information that you can offer concerning her possible further movements would be appreciated.'

The policeman shook his honest thatch of hair and said, 'Sir, other than she seemed to want urgently to get to Steyning I don't know how I can help you. There is no train direct from here to Steyning. She would need to travel to Brighton and then take two further trains to get there. One of the cabs could have took her, but I doubt if the half-sovereign that we loaned her would have covered it.'

We thanked him, and as we left the police station Holmes said, 'I believe the sergeant underestimates the young woman's enterprise; we, however, know her a little better. If Ilona wanted to reach Steyning then reach it she would. It is also entirely possible that she used the money from the distress fund to improve and change her appearance. Half a sovereign should have stretched to that.'

We returned to the railway station and questioned a couple of the cab drivers. The first said that the previous day had been a quiet one and that no single lady had got into his vehicle. But he thought that he had seen a woman with a red shawl and white gloves climb into the cab of his rival, a Mr Higgins. The latter proved helpful in supplying details of his journey with the lady with the red shawl who indeed had desired to go to Steyning.

'I said I would have to charge her fifteen shillings on account of my having to come all the way back. But she told me that she had a friend at the King's Head public house, which is nearer to Bramber than Steyning, who would pay me a sovereign when we got there. She spoke well, sir, and so I took the chance and took her there.'

'Would you like to earn another sovereign and take us there?'

Holmes's invitation was snapped up. 'Climb in, gents, I'll have you there in no time.'

The driver's natural knowledge of the winding Sussex lanes was sharpened by recent experience as he took us through Hurstpierpoint and Henfield, and eventually to Bramber. I could not remember being in the delightful little town before but tried to make a mental note to visit it again when there was no pressing reason to do so. The King's Head bore a hanging sign in the shape of a portrait of Charles the Second.

At the sight of this, as the cab made its way back to Burgess Hill, Sherlock turned to me and spoke quietly. 'Who taught you history at Greyfriars, Watson?'

Several different form masters, Wigg, Capper, Prout, but it was the history as expounded by Mr Quelch that I remember most clearly, from my days in the Remove. Quelch was a real old tartar but he could tell a good story.'

'Did he have any good stories about Charles the Second, I mean concerning the period when his forces were fighting those of Cromwell?'

I brightened and I remembered the stories of Charles hiding in an oak tree.

I said, 'There was something about him escaping to France from an inn called the King's . . .'

I trailed off as Holmes chuckled and took up the story. 'Called the King's Head after the event, of course. But it was near Bramber, and had a cellar which adjoined the River Adur. Charles was smuggled out of that cellar in a small boat which took him down the river and out to sea at Shoreham. Unlikely as it sounds he was able to reach the French coast.'

I started, 'You mean you think Ilona may have flown the coop the same way?'

'History has a way of repeating itself, my dear Watson!'

We decided not to enter the inn because we could have encountered the quarry. I felt at first that there was little chance of this, believing that if she had meant to emulate King Charles she would already have done so.

But Holmes pointed out the tidal situation to me; the Adur being still tidal at this point. 'If my navigational knowledge is still active, Watson, she would have missed last night's tide, so we must watch to see if she takes advantage of tonight's. There are bushes on the opposite bank and we can get a good view of any hidden boathouse being brought into use. What o'clock do you make it?'

'Six and ten minutes.'

'Then we have perhaps an hour to alert the police, for we cannot take the full responsibility regarding what has to be done.'

From the local police station they were able to connect us with Mycroft by telephone. I was amazed that this was possible considering the distance involved, but was to learn later that only Mycroft's unique position did indeed make this practical. His voice was as clear as a bell, where on the public telephone system it would have been extremely distorted. Holmes was able to hold the earpiece in such a position that I too could hear what was said. As nearly as memory serves the conversation was thus . . .

'Hello, brother mine. I have located the quarry.'

'Well done, but have you apprehended her?'

'No, and my reason is that I have the germ of an idea that might result in the discovery of a whole crowd of enemy agents.'

'Pray give me details, Sherlock.'

'She is at an inn at Bramber in Sussex, the King's Head, which has a partly submerged access to the Adur from which Charles the Second escaped Cromwell, by way of

Shoreham harbour. She would have left last evening were it not for the tide being wrong. Tonight it is right and if my calculations are correct she will try in about an hour.'

'The Germans will have a boat of some kind waiting for her, doubtless?'

'I imagine so. Mycroft, there is little time; listen carefully to what I intend to do. We will watch to see if she emerges in a boat. If she does we will apprehend her with the help of the local police. They will then go into the inn and find out if it is the nest of vipers that I suspect. If so they will be busy, and there will be no time to waste to catch the tide. I will be in the small boat in place of Ilona, Watson too if there is room. We will explain that she has been apprehended and that we are her colleagues.'

'You think they will believe you?'

'I consider that I know enough details of her background, hers and Brand's, to get away with it. They will grill me for details of the planned movements of forces on the Western Front. As I have no knowledge of these I cannot give anything away and might well be able to mislead them. But more important, I may learn who their agents are in France, and much else to our advantage.'

'If you think you can get away with it, you have my blessing. Contact our embassy in Paris when you are able; I will be in touch with them. Please remember, Sherlock, that you will be taking on an enterprise where our French allies might be suspicious of you. You will be on French territory at least, or so I imagine, but the Germans you deal with will still be dangerous.'

Holmes was irritatingly casual in his final words to Mycroft. 'We are both stoutly shod, and Watson has his service revolver! Oh, by the way, will you retrieve our baggage from the Golden Lion in Burgess Hill and pay the landlord whatever he feels he is owed?'

The Holmes brothers tied up a few details and then we led a police party towards the King's Head, for time and tide wait for no man.

CHAPTER FIVE

'The Game is Afloat!'

A slightly bewildered police Inspector Garstang with a Sergeant Wilson and several constables, two of them in plain clothes, accompanied us to the King's Head. The latter were sent into the public bar of the inn, to behave as patrons until the right moment arrived. Holmes and I led the inspector to a vantage place behind the bushes on the far bank. Two constables were sent to a spot upon the bank beside the inn. They were in gumboots. The river was neither wide nor deep at this point.

After what felt like hours but was only about thirty minutes in fact, a flap at the partly submerged side of the building was raised, and a boat dropped, or I suppose I should say, slithered crablike into the waters of the Adur. It was obvious that the cellar from which it emerged was partly submerged. It was almost dark, but we could see what was happening. Doubtless given a more suitable tidal situation our quarry would have waited until the black of night. I could just make out the figure of Ilona as she scrambled into the craft, which appeared to be some sort of a skiff. There were oars which she would scarcely need, as the tidal water would take her to the river mouth. Garstang, nudged by Holmes, blew sharply upon his whistle and the two constables waded around to apprehend Ilona and prevent the boat from floating down the Adur.

The lady put up quite a struggle but was soon handcuffed and on dry land. The boat was safely tied up and we all made for the little bridge which led us near the entrance to the inn. We entered the bar into which the plain clothes men had been sent, to find the landlord being restrained by them.

He was very vociferous in his protestations. 'Can't a bloke go about his normal business without being invaded by a gang of rozzers?'

Holmes spoke quickly and sharply. 'We are here to intercept your normal business which involves treacherous acts, involving the safety of the realm. Take us to your cellars. If you cooperate with us, who knows, it might even prevent the judge from putting on the black cap at your trial!'

With muttered curses he led us down some steps and into a cellar cool and typical of a three-hundred-year-old hostelry. There were wine racks and barrels, but Holmes could not see what he was seeking. Then he suddenly brightened as he clutched at one of the large racks of bottles which lined one wall. With my help and that of a policeman he moved it, and we found that it opened like a door. He pointed at a semi-circular scar upon the floor, rather like that made by an ill-fitting door in a house.

'That arc showed me which was the rack to inspect! See, there are further steps and the river laps below. I'll wager this secret river exit has remained untouched since King Charles used it.'

But Holmes was seeking something else: he looked around the cellar with darting bird-like glances. Eventually he pointed to a barrel which stood on end beside a row of others. A certain amount of experiment enabled him to open the top and reveal what I can only describe as a false compartment in the top end, containing a morse key.

'You see, Inspector, this barrel owes more to Marconi than to the hop fields of Kent.'

'I noticed you made straight for that barrel, yet it looks identical to the others, Mr Holmes.'

'True, Inspector, but the others have had frequent movement: you can see this by the circular stains at the base of each. This one has not been moved for a long time.'

I thought I knew what was in Holmes's mind. 'You will attempt to send a message to those who await Ilona?'

'Correct, Watson, and our host will give me the code name that we must contact.'

The landlord scoffed, 'What makes you think that I will do that?'

'You'll certainly make the drop if you don't. Further, my colleague and I are undertaking a dangerous mission. If we do not return from it there will be nobody to speak for you at your trial.'

The landlord gasped, every trace of colour had left his normally florid face. It was as if the prospect of being hung had only now fully registered with him.

'Very well, it is "PIERRE".'

Holmes seemed happy that this information was accurate. He turned to me. 'I understand the morse code, but I think you surpass me in that department, Watson. Contact "PIERRE" and tell him, "ILONA CAUGHT SENDING OTHERS".'

I managed to make contact with 'PIERRE' and to send the message.

Then Holmes briskly led us down to the boat and noted that there were emergency supplies aboard in the shape of bread, cheese and a water flask. 'My dear Watson, I have taken for granted your agreement to joining me in a dangerous mission. Forgive me, but in the past you have been so fearless in your alliance with me that I had forgotten the niceties of polite behaviour. Will you accompany me, my dear fellow?'

'You can depend upon me, as I am glad to hear you already knew. My country needs me, and I am happy to serve.'

My heart pumped with excitement. Having been turned down for active service I had felt rather useless and my recent involvement I had found stimulating. The hint of danger which now emerged stirred me delightfully.

Holmes conferred quickly with Inspector Garstang and in a dream-like manner I realized that we were being taken swiftly by the tide, towards the mouth of the Adur. We kept our heads down except when we needed to push the boat from the bank when it got too close.

Within the hour we were actually out to sea, and within another thirty minutes I was beginning to be a little apprehensive concerning the safety of our frail craft. I had crossed the Channel often enough, but always before in a substantial craft, and without recourse to rowing, as we now needed to do.

'Come on, Watson, you are not on the Serpentine now!'

But I noticed that Holmes caught the odd 'crab' himself! Suddenly I could hear the chug-chub of a motorized craft, and such a boat hove into sight. I might not have seen it in the dark save that it had a lamp with which it searched us out.

Holmes stood up and waved his bandana. 'Ship Ahoy! Pierre?'

'Yes, identify yourselves!'

'Colleagues of Ilona!'

The boat came very close, shutting off its engine and we manoeuvred our shell-like overgrown skiff to its side.

'Come aboard, colleagues of Ilona!'

We clambered onto the tiny deck of the motor yacht, which I for one was truly grateful to do, despite my apprehension as to what might ensue. Pierre was a large, dark man, definitely French in appearance so he was evidently a traitor rather than a patriotic German. He was hearty enough, though naturally he wanted to ensure himself that we were just what we claimed to be.

'So, you have worked with Brand and Ilona?'

'Yes, that is so!'

We were able to say this with truth and sincerity, due to our appearances in the troop concerts.

As I suspected that he might, Pierre tried to ensure our credentials by attempting to trick us in a reply. 'Brand is a marvel with his cover. He is a brilliant ventriloquist, is he not?'

Holmes replied wearily, 'That could well be true, but in our experience he is a puppeteer, which is not quite the same thing.'

'Why did Ilona not come herself; and why at this time? We were surprised to get the message.'

'She had to change her plans and those of Brand. The

Cabinet has decided that all plans for war on the Western Front will emerge from Colchester in Essex. Due to this change the information from Salisbury Plain has become unreliable.'

'So that would account for the last Stonehenge message! We thought perhaps that Brand had simply made a mistake.'

'Well in a way he did, being unaware of the change at first. But of course Brand relied entirely on the message of the spotlight. It was Johnson, obviously, who got this wrong.'

'He has gone to Chelmsford also?'

'I rather think not; perhaps he has even been found out.'

'Let us hope not, he is a good man.'

Pierre seemed happy that we were all that we claimed. I was George Mitchell, a disillusioned ex-army man, and Holmes was a similarly disillusioned scientist who rejoiced in the name of Theo Chambers. We were taken to the tiny cabin and offered hot coffee, which was indeed welcome. I realized that Holmes was extemporizing as best he could, but I wondered how long the enemy would remain unsuspicious when they received no further messages from Brand or Ilona. Alas, we had not had time to plan future movements owing to the tide situation.

Pierre explained, 'We will disembark at Dieppe if one of our own *Unterseeboots* does not get us first! Who could blame them, it would be a case of "up periscope" and "Commander, I see a French motor torpedo boat".'

Then he suddenly enquired, 'You have papers?'

Holmes used great presence of mind. 'Yes, I am impersonating a well-known celebrity to whom I bear a passing likeness. Sherlock Holmes, the celebrated detective. Mitchell looks enough like his colleague Watson to pass muster. I happen to know that Holmes has business with the British Embassy. I may beat him to it. But my friend and I have had so many aliases it is necessary to concentrate to remember just who we are supposed to be.'

Pierre chuckled. 'I know the feeling, Mr Holmes; and I will address you so from now on; I myself, despite my Gallic appearance, am actually from Alsace Lorraine, from a highly respected German family. Highly respected that is, until this war began. Now my mother goes out shopping all but shrouded. I removed myself to Dieppe where I have an antique shop, under my new name, Pierre Boyer. I have over the years established myself as a highly respectable patriot, as has my colleague Albert. We are entrusted with this motor boat as volunteer part-time coastal defence members.'

His words explained much of how he, an enemy of France, was able to be openly at sea, off the French coast. I had some misgivings concerning Holmes's cavalier use of our real personas as aliases, but he was shrewd enough for me to trust his judgement. In the days to come this trust would be proved well placed, despite many a close shave.

As predicted, we made a seemingly unextraordinary landing and Pierre was able to take us directly to his place of business. It was an unremarkable shop, double fronted, shabby and full of elderly furniture. We were introduced to his wife Yvonne who, like himself, had a very French appearance. She was dusting a davenport when we entered.

He said to her, in French, 'These gentlemen are Sherlock Holmes and Dr Watson from England. At least, those are their present identities and you will address them as such. I am taking them to the attic to see the special items.'

She nodded to us, unsmilingly, and then recommenced her dusting. She did this also without enthusiasm.

'These are the special items, and the Louis XVI wardrobe is of particular interest, gentleman.'

Pierre had led us up some stairs to the top of the four-storey building and through a clutter of old furniture. At the far side there was a large antique wardrobe which he opened. It appeared empty and uninteresting inside, for its shelves and fittings appeared to have been removed. Pierre banged upon the back of the wardrobe and that portion of it opened like a single wide door. He pulled us into the wardrobe, through this opening, and then pulled the front doors of the cabinet behind him.

'I would like this apartment to be better concealed, but at present it is the best I can manage. However, the French police and, more especially, their secret service are monumentally inefficient.'

We were in a small apartment with a sloping roof above. One wall seemed almost covered by a large map of the Western Front where pins decorated with tricolours, union flags and imperial eagles were appropriately impaled. A wireless apparatus and a morse key were on a small table. A large man, as tall as Pierre but a good deal stouter, sat in the only comfortable chair. He did not rise as we entered.

Pierre introduced us. 'Sherlock Holmes and Dr Watson, meet Voltaire. He is our commander in Dieppe; I will not bother with other names, real or otherwise.'

The fat man surveyed us critically, eventually he spoke, at last the ghost of a smile playing upon his thin lips. 'I trust you have your service revolver, Watson?'

He was not only a reader of my accounts of Holmes's exploits, but he obviously expected me to respond in a manner which would show a modicum of research into the character I was supposed to represent! The reader will realize that this was not hard for me to do.

'Not only that but we are both stoutly shod!'

He actually laughed at this reply of mine, and at Holmes's comment, 'Beware of the moors during the hours of darkness, my dear Voltaire!'

He was actually chuckling, 'So you have both done your homework well. You could easily pass as Holmes and Watson; at least for their likenesses have been depicted by Sydney Paget. What they really look like, heaven alone knows.'

Holmes chuckled. 'Heaven alone knows.'

'Well, gentlemen, to business. What went wrong with Stonehenge and where are Brand and Ilona?'

We told him what we had already recounted to Pierre. He frowned. 'I don't like the sound of this. Who do you suppose tipped off the British that they would move their HQ?'

Holmes replied with characteristic enterprise. 'Do you trust Johnson?'

'Why yes, almost as much as I trust Brand and Ilona.'

'Almost?'

His eyes narrowed. 'You have made your point, Holmes. Well, perhaps we will soon hear from them and have the situation clarified. Meanwhile, what have you to tell us that might be of interest?'

'You have heard about the new aeroplane, the one that they plan to fly at twenty thousand feet?'

'Our anti-aircraft system is so much better than theirs;

we would shoot them down before they ever reached their targets.'

'You have an anti-aircraft gun that can reach twenty thousand feet?' Holmes sounded suitably amazed, as indeed I was with his ingenuity, for what he suggested was amazing but not far enough from possibility to be quite ridiculous.

Voltaire nodded. 'You are right, such a weapon would be a disaster; we have nothing like such a plane but we will have to work on it quickly and find a way to prevent their project. I will anxiously await hearing from Ilona when she has set something up at Colchester. Meanwhile, I will have work for the pair of you, and after you have both had a good night's sleep we will talk further.'

Pierre took us to our room, over an *estaminet*, which we were to share. He bade us to try to sleep soundly to be fresh on the morrow. 'If Voltaire has work for you, be prepared for great expectations, no?'

When he had left we made sure that we were not overheard. Then we started to discuss our situation, which I for one felt to be getting far from uncomplicated.

'Holmes, we are in a situation where we are impersonating ourselves and expected to produce information for both sides!'

'Correct, Watson, but it is less involved than you make it seem. All we have to do is learn as much as we can from the German secret service for the benefit of the allies. Other than that we have only to satisfy those that we have duped that we may continue to be of value. This means that we must give them false information in exchange for real secrets. Currently we know nothing that could be of use to either side.'

'How long will the Germans, or rather their French traitors, tolerate us if we can tell the nothing?'

'My own thought entirely, Watson, and a very difficult question to answer. We could of course feed them all manner of false information, but not for long. As soon as it was realized that our information was not reliable we would either be dismissed or, worse, suspected and in consequence eliminated. What we have to do is give them some titbit that will strengthen our credibility. Meanwhile, I will have to give them something so I will invent some trifle, harmless to our cause but interesting to theirs.'

I slept but fitfully, and Holmes did not, I believe, sleep at all, for the dawn light picked him out sitting in the only easy chair that the room boasted, just as I had last seen him a little after midnight. He was smoking his pipe, and the strewn debris of tobacco ash and used vestas told their own story.

But his eyes were bright as he hailed me. 'Good morning, my dear Watson. I will not ask if you slept well because I observed your tossing and turning and heard your snores being interrupted by frequent bouts of sleeplessness.'

I grunted. 'I observe that you have not slept at all, and can only hope that lack of slumber will not dull the wits which you need very much at this time.'

'Far from that, my dear fellow, for I have been pondering the details of a plan which might save the day!'

But there was no time for further discussion because Pierre had arrived to take us to the antique shop. Once there we were given breakfast of rolls and coffee. It was explained to us that there was no butter or milk on account of the wartime conditions.

'You see, in France starvation looms, but the populace will be well fed once they have been conquered by the glorious fatherland.'

Pierre pointed to the map upon the wall and became a little more demanding than he had been thus far.

'Now, Mr Sherlock Holmes, as you had better become used to being called, what can you tell me that will be of use, aside from the news about the change of HQ in England. There must be a reason for Ilona having shown such faith in you.'

Holmes dealt with him cynically. 'Must we so soon sing for our supper? But fear not, for aside from my appointment with the British Ambassador I have a fragment which should keep you happy and busy.'

Holmes walked towards the map and extended a skeletal finger at that portion of it which involved the area around the limited German coastline near Bremer Haven.

He pointed to a small inlet and spoke with great conviction, evidently convincing Pierre, though not myself. 'The British navy cruiser *Albert Royal* will enter this inlet tomorrow at six a.m. of the clock. An armed party of British soldiers will descend in lifeboats and land nearby. If you allow the vessel to enter the mouth of the inlet before you take steps to destroy it you will prevent an attempted landing, destroy a valuable ship and eliminate perhaps a hundred British troops. The British are depending upon the element of surprise, but now that you are aware of the situation you can play them at their own game.'

Pierre was delighted with this information and was soon busy sending morse messages. Then he paused. 'Gentlemen, I believe it was a lucky day for us when we picked you up. Did you yourselves discover this piece of information?'

Holmes nodded. 'I have my methods, as Watson will tell you!'

This statement brought laughter from Pierre and his assistant in which I joined, perhaps a trifle too frenetic in its tone. I felt that Holmes was walking upon a sword-edge, but he seemed supremely confident. I could not begin to imagine what would happen on the following day when no cruiser full of soldiers, armed to the teeth, appeared upon the scene.

'Splendid. Well, I am interested only in results. If your information is proven accurate we will go full steam ahead with your visit to the embassy in Paris.'

Although there was a friendly tone in Pierre's voice, I fancied an edge to his voice suggesting that our future might be apt to hang upon the appearance of the *Albert Royal* upon the morrow.

Pierre rather accented these thoughts of mine when he dismissed us until the next day, although I had a feeling that we would be under observation. However, as we stood upon the dockside like two visitors from a friendly nation I felt it safe to converse with my friend upon that which had developed. 'Holmes, you do realize that you have got us into a fine old pickle?'

'Watson! Would I endanger our future unnecessarily?'

'So, it is necessary for us to be discovered to be just what we are and sent to a German prison to be shot? Let us go to the French authorities without delay and let them help us.'

'My dear Watson, I do not believe that we would get to talk with the authorities without being apprehended by our shadows.'

'What shadows?'

'The woman in the tweed skirt, with the poodle on a lead, and the dockside lounger in nautical garb who is in conversation with her only a hundred and fifty feet from where we stand.'

I glanced round to where his gaze had rested momentarily. I saw the characters that he had mentioned. The couple were there, seated at a roadside café. They looked for all the world like a lady of easy virtue and her quarry.

I said as much but Holmes shook his head. 'Look again, Watson, though not too openly. How is she dressed?'

I studied the woman as closely as I dared. She was dressed in somewhat flamboyant garb, rather like that worn by the street women of London's East End; a neat but loudly patterned skirt and a blouse and a jacket of similar style. Her hat was rather large and vulgar and an ostrich feather blew from it.

'I see no reason to doubt my first impression.'

'Do not look at her again, Watson, but trust my observations. She has a bracelet of diamonds; she carries several hundred pounds upon her wrist.'

'Not if the stones are imitations or cheap paste.'

'No cheap paste stones ever captured the sunlight in the manner which these do. Now tell me something about her companion.'

'He looks like a fisherman home from the sea and seeking female companionship.'

'How is he attired?'

'Why, in a smock and canvas breeches, with a sailor's peaked cap.'

'How about his feet?'

'I did not notice . . .'

'Exactly. As so often you looked but failed to take in what you saw. He is wearing a pair of boots that would not be out of place in Bond Street. Do not be ashamed of your lack of astute observation for they are equally lax in their disguise.'

I had to admit the logic of his observations. But this shrewdity on the part of Sherlock Holmes hardly seemed to be much help to our situation. I repeated my belief that we would be in peril on the morrow when the naval manoeuvre failed to materialize.

But Holmes, as so often in the past, dropped his bombshell. 'The information which I gave Pierre concerning the *Albert Royal* entering that inlet was correct in most of its details.'

'What?' I could not believe that he spoke these words.

'Just a bit of information that I picked up at the HQ on Salisbury Plain, whilst you were doubtless wasting your time.'

'You mean to say that the *AR* will enter the inlet at six a.m. on the morrow?'

'It will indeed, Watson, it will indeed.'

'But Holmes, what have you done? Why, the Germans have been alerted and will be waiting in ambush!'

Holmes was amused by my words. 'Watson, they will get just what they expect, the *Albert Royal*, which will be at their mercy and they will blow it up! But no British lives will be lost because the ship will be empty save for a cargo of explosives. You see, the poor old *AR* is past its time of use to the Royal Navy. The plan was therefore to tow it to the inlet and let the tide take it further. When it blows up, as it will by plan, there will be no one aboard, and the inlet will be rendered unnavigable for weeks! If the Germans blow it up they will only be hastening the event by an hour or so. By warning the Germans I have additionally tied up quite a large force that might otherwise be engaging our forces on the Western Front!'

I could see how Holmes had turned the intended blockage of the inlet to something more effective and cemented belief in our loyalty to Pierre.

I admit that my manner towards Holmes was somewhat subdued for some time after. How could I have ever doubted his loyalty to his country, his good sense and sagacity in using a chance piece of knowledge to our advantage? It would be a long time before I doubted him again.

We sauntered around, performing very normal actions in entering shops to make purchases, having first visited a bank to exchange our pounds for francs. Every now and again we sighted the couple who were evidently keeping an eye on us.

Everywhere we went we were greeted with a subdued friendliness from the local population as soon as they realized our nationality. Subdued because although they were our allies the French had taken the brunt of the losses in men, horses, and even civilians, in fighting the war to end all wars, against a foe with superior arms, one that had anticipated the conflict longer than any.

We of course had no ration tickets which would enable us to buy staple foodstuffs in the shops but we soon realized that, as in England, these were not required to eat in cafés. This solved our immediate problems and we were able to purchase the necessities of life which we lacked through our sudden departure from England, home and beauty!

That evening we returned to our room and were visited there by Pierre. He was charming enough, though with that hint of menace that could only be detected after having been in his company for a while. 'So, Mr Holmes, Dr Watson, you will be accompanied to my little HQ first thing tomorrow morning. You can breakfast with me again and we will discuss future plans commensurate with events, yes?'

I tried to act as casually as Holmes appeared to. A thousand doubts crossed my mind 'what if' this and 'what if' that, but mainly 'What if the British decided to cancel the destruction of the *Albert Royal*?' After all, they had no idea that our future depended upon it!

Holmes spoke to me his echoes of my doubts and fears as soon as we were alone again. 'It is almost certain that the British navy will carry out their plan but in the unlikely occurrence that they do not it is well that we are prepared. Of course, we could at this point take a stroll and disappear into the night, but if we do so although it would ensure our safety it would yet lose for our country some vital piece of information that might provide a revival in our fortunes of war. I leave the decision to you, Watson; I feel I should not allow you to endanger your life without careful and considered thought.'

Of course he knew, I think, what my answer would be. 'If there is the slightest chance that we can learn something to the advantage of the allied cause, there is no doubt in my mind that we should see this thing through. But if it results in a tight corner, Holmes, shall we attempt to bluff or fight our way out of it? I have my revolver still.'

'I feel that under such an unlikely situation bluff would

be our best weapon, but I applaud your patriotism, Watson, and if it does come to a fight there is no man I would sooner have at my side. Come, old friend, we have extricated each other from a dozen death-threatening situations. I sometimes feel that we lead charmed lives, you and I. Let us throw the whole thing from our minds and go to the *estaminet* opposite for some bread and cheese and wine. Our shadows may watch us, but we will given them no cause for suspicion.'

I was amazed at the variety of comestibles that one could still order from a wayside French *estaminet*; a splendid choice of cheeses, for example, and we could have eaten escalope of veal had we so wished, whereas in England we would have been offered fish, sausages or rissoles, with the additional words at the slightest curl of the lip, 'Don't you know there's a war on?' I suppose our regular shadows had to sleep or rest sometimes, for there were two fresh ones watching us. Holmes soon spotted the plumber with the bag of tools at one of the other tables, ostensibly chatting with a sporty-looking sort in a striped jersey and flat cap.

'You will observe, Watson, that the plumber's attire is immaculate as if straight from his wife's washtub. He has his tools with him. At this hour he would normally have finished his day's work and his attire would show that. His only other reason for being abroad with his tools would be an emergency, at such an hour as this, yet he is obviously in no hurry to depart and half of Dieppe would perhaps be flooded by now if the responsibility were his!'

'How about the sporting gentleman?'

'He looks, I'll grant you, of that fraternity, yet he is holding a racing paper fully three days old. He will pick few winners from that, which is what he appears to be trying to do.'

'I know you have eyes like a hawk, Holmes, but can you read the date on that newspaper at such a distance?'

'No, Watson, but like so many other sporting papers this one presents a headline of more general news upon its front page. The event referred to is easily read even by yourself.'

I had to agree that the newspaper headline referred to an incident which had occurred whilst we were still safely in England. I changed the subject. 'This could be our last meal together, Holmes!'

'True, Watson, but what better for a last meal than a slice of camembert with fresh rolls and a glass of moselle? Moreover, I can think of no better company in which to partake of it.'

But our lurking fears were groundless for on the morrow Pierre greeted us with joyful enthusiasm. 'Thanks to you, Mr Holmes (forgive me if I continue to thus address you), our gallant forces have destroyed the cruiser *Albert Royal*, evidently along with all on board. It would seem that a shot or two from our concealed cannon was enough to blow the whole ship into countless pieces with blaze that could be seen for miles. I wonder if perhaps there was some new weapon being carried, for I doubt if the cannon alone could have caused such devastation!'

Holmes was daring in his next question I felt. 'What of the landing party?'

'Impossible to say; no sign of anyone emerging and they must of course all have been blown to kingdom come. But investigation of the wreckage will give the answer to this and other questions. Have some coffee and rolls . . . there is a special treat for you . . . some honey.'

Perhaps still thinking a trap was not out of the question I said, 'The real Sherlock Holmes may be an apiarist, but I do not think my friend is any judge of honey.'

I had said the right thing; Pierre simply saying, 'Your homework has been good. It would hardly do for "Dr Watson" to be unaware of Holmes's hives; he has mentioned them often in his writings. I imagine you have read all of the exploits in *The Strand*?'

I could truthfully reply that I had.

But then a rather more worrying turn of events occurred. Pierre spoke of our intended visit to the embassy in Paris.

'I suggest you make your proposed rendezvous with the British at the embassy as soon as possible. You can falsely alert them to a completely new tactic, a German invasion of the south of France which, if you are convincing, may tie up quite a large allied force and leave the field clear for Operation Short Cut: you will have been told the details of this as you are colleagues of Ilona so I hardly need to tell you when and where this will be. So the best of luck, Mr Sherlock Holmes, may you and the good doctor serve us well with your visit. Aside from matters we have discussed I know you will keep your eyes and ears open for things in general.'

We were on the Paris-bound train, along with what seemed like half the population of France. There were peasant women with baskets, doubtless lured by the high prices to be got for their home-produced vegetables and poultry in the capital. There were French soldiers with their waxed moustaches and high colour, with their kit bags, returning to the Western Front by way of Paris.

There were also persons who glanced around them with suspicion, for the atmosphere was tense in this country which had come so near to defeat as to produce many who would consider becoming traitors to the cause in return for the ultimate safety of themselves and their families. We had not experienced this in Britain and I imagine the Channel between us and the European mainland had given us a sense of insulation and isolation, producing a perhaps false bravado.

Holmes had decided that we were free of any shadows. 'I believe we have passed our first hurdle. It is a pity that we may not be able to return and take further advantage. I feel, Watson, that our next scene of investigation might be upon the Western Front itself.'

We discussed of course that tantalizing code name, all that we had been able to learn of Operation Short Cut. At least this is what I believed until Holmes told me that he thought he had some idea of the area where it might involve itself.

'I did see a marked area on the map, right in the centre of the forest of the Ardenne, but I dared not chance my arm further, as you know.'

We arrived without appointment at the embassy but were admitted upon the presentation of our cards, and ushered as if expected up the ornate staircase and eventually taken to an almost equally ornate office. It was a large apartment with a huge bay window looking out upon a rear garden, its doubtless normally ornate drapes had been replaced by those of heavy black cloth, it being the more necessary in Paris to shade lights than in London through the proximity of the enemy and frequency of air raids.

These curtains had been gathered up at each side of the window to admit daylight. They were substantial and floor length.

Behind a huge desk sat an aide to the Ambassador and he rose to greet us, bowing and indicating the two large leather-covered chairs on our side of the desk. 'Mr Holmes, Dr Watson, I have of course been expecting you and am relieved that you are both safe.'

After a few returned niceties, Holmes, much to my amazement, raised his voice to say, 'You can come out now, Mycroft!'

I started, and there was a stirring of one of the gathered black drapes. Amazingly it had hidden the vast bulk of Sherlock's older brother. He asked of Sherlock, 'The aroma of my special Havana?'

The younger brother replied, 'That and the depression that your nether area had made on the leather of the seat. It is unmistakable, rather like a vast fingerprint! There was one other thing which cemented the belief in your presence.'

'Which was?'

'The toe-caps of your boots, specially made for you by Chapple of St James's. He makes the ventilation holes distinct to each client. But upon my word, what on earth could possibly stir you from your armchair at the Diogenes that could possibly involve me?'

His deep irony was not lost on Mycroft Holmes who flung himself into a chair near a side wall. 'Brother mine, our continued interrogation of Brand and Ilona have led me to believe that you might have been getting yourselves into an extremely dangerous situation. Pierre, who you will by now know well, is an extremely dangerous man. If he had suspected your real identities you would not be here now.'

Sherlock, with my interpolation here and there, told Mycroft everything that had occurred since we had left the King's Head. The ambassador's aide found the narrative as fascinating as Mycroft undoubtedly did.

'Well done, little brother, we have not only blocked a valuable German access to the North Sea, but thanks to you we have gained troop movement and anxiety from it. As for Operation Short Cut, we knew of this by title, but your observation regarding the Ardenne is valuable to us. We are puzzled as to the character that it will have. A short cut can mean a detour but I'm inclined to think that it might be concerned with aircraft dropping infantry from the skies, some kind of vastly advanced parachutes that their backroom johnnies might have come up with. In view of your information regarding the Ardenne we can at least move reinforcements to that area.'

But Sherlock Holmes shook his head. 'Pray do not draw attention yet to the fact that we know the likely location. Let me try to learn more before you take action.'

'Wise, as ever, Sherlock, I will confer with the commander-in-chief. Meanwhile, I will furnish you with documents which will give you a more or less free hand.'

A typewriter operator was sent for, and as Mycroft dictated she keyed in his words with her deft fingers.

Finally he signed it and placed a seal upon it. 'There, Sherlock, that seal will frighten the life out of any commanding officer or intelligence aide. I will be staying here until you are able to accompany me safely home. You can reach me through a special telephone line, or by morse to the radio room. By the way, the French authorities should cooperate with you at the sight of that seal.'

I could not resist asking, 'What method of transportation brought you here, Mycroft?'

'Aeroplane!'

I could tell from the mirthless tone of his voice that he was not attempting to be humorous.

Sherlock Holmes dropped his bombshell, at least it was one as far as I was concerned. 'Watson and I will need to use that method of transportation.'

Mycroft did not start or flinch, indeed was wide eyed as he replied, 'You will need two planes; those we have available are two-seaters and one of the seats is of course for the pilot. Even you, with all your talents, cannot be trusted to pilot a plane: to train you would take weeks.'

Sherlock nodded with understanding. 'Very well, we will use two planes, for I wish Watson to observe the Ardenne just as I will; an extra pair of eyes is of great assistance.'

CHAPTER SIX

Over the Ardenne

I will spare the reader many tiresome details: enough at this point to tell you that Holmes and I found ourselves each in the rear cockpit of a separate aeroplane. It was not my first flight in such a machine, but the first under wartime conditions. This hazardous situation, however, was counteracted to some extent by the progress that had been made in the design and building of aircraft since our adventure with *The Man Who Lost Himself.* The two young men who piloted us were both remarkably casual, their neckerchiefs unfurling in the breeze as we took off. Both our aircraft circled the field a couple of times until Holmes's plane led in the direction we wanted.

In an incredibly short time, or so it seemed, we were buffeting over the great forest which was our goal. I knew what to look for because Holmes and I had discussed it at length. We were seeking a place in the forest where there was a clearing, large enough for an aircraft to land, for we had not ruled out Operation Short Cut being concerned with a newly invented air machine which could land and spill forth a number of armed soldiers. Several such machines, landing in turn, could, given the element of surprise, deliver a very telling blow to the allies so far behind the front line.

As I narrowed my eyelids I spied no large clearings, though there were quite a few smaller ones largely caused by enemy shelling. We hovered over that vast forest for quite a long time before I spotted a rather larger clearing than those we had seen before. Perhaps not large enough for a plane to land but practical for the dropping of soldiers by parachute; a ruse which would not be very sensible where no clearings were involved as the tent-like accessories would catch upon trees and dangle the participants like minnows. Moreover, our regular patrols would soon spot them . . . unless . . . I started to think of a night drop, with tree-green parachutes and equipped with rope ladders! But I made a mental note not to tell my thoughts to Holmes for fear of ridicule. Yet my curiosity made me wish to see this clearing at closer quarters and I leaned over and asked the pilot if he could swoop low that I might see more. He raised a thumb and started a series of elliptical descents and ascents for my convenience.

Alas, as the sky started to spin, as did my insides as well. I realized that the pilot was not showing off with aerobatics, rather we were in really serious trouble. It occurred to me that we were going to crash as soon as we had hit the single tallest tree. There was a shudder and an enormous crash and we were perched between two trees, our wings entangled in half a hundred branches at a terrifying height. Of course there was a good view of the clearing, but this was not our main concern any more.

I had not climbed about in trees since my schooldays when the elms at Greyfriars had been fairly important in my life. But I was not bird-nesting now, or even using a tree as an aid to climbing a wall, rather was I trying to use a tree as a ladder of descent to terra firma. The young pilot managed it quite well and he reached the ground long before me, offering advice both practical and impractical. But in spite of, rather than on account of, his help I did reach the ground with no worse injuries than a few scratches.

The pilot apologised to me. 'Sorry, Dr Watson, but please do not worry, the pilot in Mr Holmes's plane will soon spot where our plane is wedged and help will soon be here.'

'What form will that help take?' I was anxious.

'An armoured motor car will make for the nearest spot on a road, and then a ground party will come and find us. We could probably find the road ourselves, but we could get thoroughly lost and there are boars and even bears in the forest.'

I made certain that I had not dropped my revolver during my undignified descent but I soon felt the reassuring bulge under my jacket.

'Boars eh, bears eh, it is beginning to sound like the stock exchange what, only need a few bulls!' Then I remembered having read of an all but extinct European buffalo, the Wissant, and began to hope that it was indeed extinct!

The talk of the road made me remember something rather strange that I had noted from the air. I had fancied I could see parallel lines leading partly across the clearing.

I mentioned this to the pilot who explained, 'From high above, from a plane, you can often see that which is just below the surface which cannot be seen from close to. For example, buried Roman villas have often been detected from aircraft.'

'I see. So I may have seen an ancient road which has been long covered by soil?'

'Something like that.'

It was perhaps half an hour before the rescue party arrived, with Holmes all but leading it.

'That was very careless of you, Watson. Do you realize that you have destroyed a valuable aeroplane? We are here to aid the war effort, not the opposite! Well, anyway I am glad you are safe.'

I must have looked really glum, because my pilot said, 'Don't worry, Doctor, it happens all the time. New set of wings and the machine will fly again.'

But I was feeling sorry for myself because I said, somewhat sulkily, 'Well anyway, Holmes, I did possibly discover a forgotten road; maybe Roman, you know.'

I explained the phenomenon of the distant aerial view showing tracks where none seemed to exist. Holmes was, to my surprise, rather interested. He tramped around the clearing and searched for what I said that I had seen. However, we could not find it.

Holmes turned to his pilot, 'Do you think you could fly over again and help us to pinpoint this phenomenon that Dr Watson has described?'

The intrepid bird-man agreed to try to help us and within fifteen minutes or so we were treated to the sight of what I could still view as seeming like an enormous box-kite hovering as slowly as it was able overhead. The plane returned, swooped, departed and then swooped again. This time the pilot appeared to be leaning out of his cockpit as he hurled a small white object towards the ground. As it made contact it burst, leaving a small mushroom-shaped cloud which descended to leave a white deposit over the scrubby turf. It had in fact been a bag of flour!

Our pilot joined us as we viewed the white burst on the grass. He said, 'Old Havers usually has the odd flour bag in his plane; practical joker you know, drops them on our own airfields just to show how easy it would be for the enemy to do the same with bombs!'

Holmes was, however, more concerned with the accuracy of the flour bomb than the reason for its availability. 'I imagine we must wait for Havers to rejoin us to know just how accurate he has been. He will be in a better position to know, but there is no harm in taking a preliminary look.'

Holmes walked around the white debris and viewed it at a distance from all angles. He stopped his eyes down like a photographer might adjust the iris diaphragm of his lens. But eventually he was content to sit upon a tree stump, smoking his clay and awaiting the return of Flying Officer Havers. I could see, however, that he was very deep in thought.

When Havers returned he was full of enthusiasm, pointing to the white star on the green grass with excitement. 'Mr Holmes, I scored a very accurate hit. When I returned and swooped low I could not only see the parallel lines that Dr Watson had described but I could see that my flour bomb was so accurate that the edges of the flour almost touched the lines on each side.'

I always err on the side of pessimism, I suppose, saying, 'Of course, this may indeed be only some ancient remains, or if not it could be something that our people would rather have remain uncovered.'

Holmes leapt to his feet, knocked his pipe on the stump and, once sure that it was inactive, returned it to his pocket. 'Oh come, Watson, if we discover something that we should not we can conceal it again without having done much harm. I am not going to waste the time which consultation with HQ would entail. Tell me, Watson, what length would you say the lines were?'

'Twenty, thirty feet . . . it is hard to judge from on high.'

But Havers agreed. 'Right on target, Doctor; I am more used to judging distance from above, but I would put the length at about twenty-four feet.'

Holmes enquired of him, 'We have established that your strike was accurate, between the lines so to speak; but Havers, how near to one or other end was it?'

Havers walked over to the flour, then paced a few feet to the west of it. 'Very roughly speaking, the lines ceased at about this point. My strike was well to the western end of its length.'

Sherlock Holmes nodded and called for the sergeant who had driven him near to this clearing. 'Driver, could I trouble you to return to your vehicle and fetch that which I feel sure you have aboard it; a British army bayonet?'

The sergeant saluted, spun upon his axis and marched off as smartly as the trees and shrubs would allow.

'Upon my word, these military people take things a little too seriously. I don't know how you managed to endure it, Watson.'

But Holmes was as anxious as anyone to proceed with his labours. Until the sergeant returned with the bayonet he spent his time sharpening a stick which he had fashioned from a fallen branch and then marking two parallel scars, each a few feet long, on each side of the flour spill. He made another scar to join them at about the place where Havers insisted that the lines had ceased. He tried to push the sharpened stick into the grass-covered earth but it resisted his efforts and I began to understand why he wanted the bayonet.

When the sergeant returned with the required weapon Holmes lost little time in putting it to use. Using all his strength he drove it into the earth, near to where he predicted the one extremity of that which we were investigating lay.

There were beads of perspiration on his brow as he withdrew the blade. 'As I suspected, there is a wooden barrier about eighteen inches below the surface.'

He repeated his action in several other places and nodded with satisfaction. 'The wooden surface is quite extensive. What we must do now is to remove some of the turf and topsoil in order to find what it is.'

Holmes loosened a section of turf, about a yard square, with the bayonet, and we dug it out with a piece of metal from the crashed aeroplane. I noticed that Holmes placed this square, although it was broken into several pieces, carefully to one side. He had revealed what he suspected, an area of wood, in fact a series of planks. These were firm enough, denoting strong bearers below. We worked like beavers to remove more turf to find that the planks ended very close indeed to the markers that Holmes had made. Then, working back the opposite way, we discovered that we were dealing with a large trap door.

'What do you make of it, Watson?'

'Some sort of ancient burial place?'

'Hardly, for the planks from which it is fashioned are recent and free from any sort of rot, so their placing here is also current. There is only one way that we can find out more and that is to endeavour to open this primitive flap. It is very heavy and I doubt if we can do it without help.'

It was decided that the sergeant should return to his HQ, taking the two pilots, one to return to his plane and the other to inform his commander of the state of his aircraft. The sergeant would return with some strong infantrymen with spades and levers.

Holmes said to them by way of farewell, 'I need hardly say, gentlemen, that at this early stage discretion is essential. Tell only those who you must, and swear them to secrecy. I know that I can rely upon you.'

When they had gone we sat and rested from our labours which had used in both of us long-neglected muscles. We knew that the party we expected by return would bring food and drink.

Meanwhile we consoled our appetites with strong tobacco as Holmes quietly pondered the happenings of the past couple of hours. 'Watson, if we have discovered anything of importance we have you to thank for it. Your eyes are keen still, especially for a man of your years, and few would have noticed those parallel lines from the air. Well, we have not, I feel, discovered the remains of a Roman villa, but we could have discovered something of equal importance, at least to the future of our cause.'

Then he was silent for several minutes, with a silence that I knew better than to disturb.

Eventually he continued, 'Operation Short Cut . . . I wonder, could it be possible?'

'Could what be possible, to what do you refer?'

'Watson, I have a thought so wild that I hardly dare to take it seriously myself. Therefore I will defer confiding it even to you until I have more to substantiate it. You know that wild speculation sometimes changes to known fact. But it is better to have some evidence to bolster up one's inspiration. But we will soon see if my practical work is still as strong as that which is theoretical.'

He said little more and I decided not to disturb his reverie, leaving this to the return of the sergeant with a trio of brawny soldiers bearing various implements. With spades they stripped back more turf to reveal a join which further investigation revealed to be roughly hinged. The huge flap was raised, first with levers and eventually by sheer muscle power. As this flap was double backwards it revealed a space below it, rather like the entrance to a mineshaft. The party had brought a lamp which showed us more than we could have seen without it. The void was about six feet deep and it was decided that one of us should drop inside and investigate further. The sergeant volunteered to do this, but Holmes shook his head. 'You are a good fellow, Sergeant but I need to inspect what is down there in my own way.'

Holmes made the short drop, taking the lamp and a small khaki bag.

His last words to me were, 'Should I be gone for some time, Watson, do not attempt to follow. I have no way of knowing quite how large the underground space may be, but I will investigate as best I can. If practical, I will return within the hour.'

I found his words surprising, as if he thought that some sort of tunnel was involved, where only a subterranean chasm was obvious as far as we could know. However, we obeyed his instructions and could only wait and speculate when he had failed to reappear within half an hour.

At this point the sergeant was inclined to ignore Holmes's instructions, opining that the detective could have been trapped or crushed by falling earth, boards or other debris. But I managed to restrain him. He recognized the old army man that stood before him and obeyed. I had formed my own plan in that I would myself descend into the chasm and investigate if Holmes did not return by sunset.

However, I did not need to do so: just as the sun was making a farewell beyond the trees I heard the familiar incisive voice. 'Watson, tell the others to be silent, and speak yourself in the softest of tones. I have much to report, so please help me up, there's a good fellow.'

I put a finger to my lips as I glanced around at our little party, then I helped my friend to return from beneath mother earth. He was very much stained with dirt and tossed the khaki bag to one side.

Then, speaking almost in a whisper, he said, 'Come, gentlemen, we must put everything back as it was. Be patient and I will tell you of my findings soon enough, but first we must make the restoration.'

In near silence we all laboured to lower the stout wood flap and cover it with earth and turf, imitating as nearly as we could that which we had first found. No golf course devotees had ever quite so lovingly stamped down the replaced divots. Finally, when Holmes was satisfied that all traces of flour had been removed ('That the spot may not seem to have altered, even in the eyes of German pilots'), Holmes began to tell us of his discovery, though he returned the soldiers to the vehicle before he spoke. 'Watson, what I dropped into was simply the entrance to a very long, extremely crude tunnel.'

'Where does it lead, do you suppose?'

'Had I been able to follow it to its termination I could answer that question, but that was not practical. The further I followed it the greater the risk of my being detected by the enemy.'

'You mean that the tunnel was constructed by the Germans?'

'I do indeed!'

'But how could that be? Surely it could not be long enough to have originated on their side of the battlefields?'

'I mean just that, Watson. If you look inside the khaki bag you will find a number of artefacts that I found, only partially covered by traces of soil. A trowel, with the name of a German manufacturer imprinted upon it, some cigarette ends, of a brand most readily available to the German armed forces, and also a small sack of soil with a fragment of rope attached to it. Please do not take my word, but examine these items for yourself.'

I opened the khaki bag and found that everything within it was just as he had described.

But I felt bound to question him upon the implications which he seemed to advance. 'But Holmes, whilst I agree that everything seems to point to some German workmen having laboured within the tunnel I find it impossible to believe that they had started to dig from their own side of the battlefields!'

My friend waxed enigmatic as he replied, 'You have too soon forgotten your boyhood reading, Watson. Do you not recall how Edmund Dantes and the Abbé Faria laboured for years to dig their way out of the Château d'If? They took so long because they had home-made tools and purloined spoons, and there were only two of them.'

'But Holmes, that was merely fiction by Alexander Dumas!'

'Truth is often stranger than fiction, old friend, and Dumas invariably based his fiction upon truths, half-truths and legends, did he not? I have known many cases of tunnelling that would make this one seem to be quite a commonplace affair. The wonder is that they have managed to finish this one, right into their enemy's territory; and it would be undiscovered still had your sharp eyes not spotted those lines which can only be located from the air.'

I was happy to think that I had been of service, but was still a little puzzled as to the ultimate use to which this access might be put.

Holmes explained his belief. 'Operation Short Cut does not refer to an attack from above, or any kind of detour or pincer movement, but an actual invasion from the bowels of the earth. Just think, Watson, they would have the advantage of surprise. They would be pouring into French territory in huge numbers before their presence could be detected. They could even make an attack from the rear upon the French army, and their land forces could attack to coincide. This discovery may have saved the allies from a possible final humiliating defeat. We must act quickly now, and contact Mycroft with all possible speed.'

We returned to the vehicle and were soon upon the field

telephone to Sherlock's influential brother. Sherlock Holmes conveyed all of the information that had been discovered, along with his theories and suggestions for prompt action. This meant that a substantial force was sent to the forest to be hidden in readiness for the suspected secret attack.

Mycroft considered that any return to Dieppe upon our parts was unwise. He explained, 'We are ready for them now, and if, or when, this infiltration occurs we will round up the entire coterie of traitors. You have performed wonders, both of you, and the time has come for you to return to England, home and beauty, what?'

We were flown home in two biplanes, very shaky but the only aircraft that could be spared. It was about ten days later that Holmes, who had decided to put up at the Charing Cross Hotel until we got some definite news, telephoned me to enquire if I had seen the newspaper headlines. I had, and arranged to meet him for lunch at Simpson's. Over a slice of game pie and a few potatoes we discussed events. From the reports in the more reliable newspapers it seemed that the Germans had in fact attempted to invade French territory by way of the tunnel. The hidden army that awaited them killed a hundred German infantry and had taken even more prisoners. Moreover, a mile or so of the tunnel had been detonated, where French sappers had secretly placed explosives. This action killed more German soldiers and effectively blocked off the tunnel, making its future use impossible. Moreover, aerial watchers had detected a massing of troops at the German entrance to the warren which led to bombardment of the survivors who tried to exit the tunnel on the enemy side.

I perhaps need hardly mention to the discerning reader

that this engagement marked a turning point in the allies' fortunes on the Western Front. When the Americans entered the conflict it was a welcome bonus rather than the miraculous life-saving event that had been hoped for. I must be fair and say that the Germans carried on hostilities bravely against eventual overwhelming odds. But then they could have avoided the whole episode could they not, or rather the Kaiser could have. By the time it ended on 11 November 1918 he was busy chopping wood at his retreat in Holland. As far as I know he is still at it, and we have discovered that the Germans are quite nice chaps after all! Certainly we are never likely to go to war with each other again.

The next time we saw Mycroft was at the Diogenes in the summer of 1918. By this time he had acquired a military rank to add to his many other establishment qualifications. He wore a British army uniform, rather like that of a general, but I never did discover what his actual rank was.

'All over, bar the shouting, what? Well, it really was the war to end all wars; the leading nations have learned a savage lesson and I have been asked to aid in the formation of a league of nations which will solve all friction by diplomacy and common sense.'

Sherlock gave his brother a rather patronizing glance. When he eventually spoke, it was with great sincerity, even if his views were somewhat misguided. 'My dear Mycroft, in most ways you surpass even my not inconsiderable mental powers of deduction and detection. But I fear that you will have a touching belief in the common sense of human nature. *Homo sapiens* is a predator and essentially competitive en masse. You are right in so much as none of us will live to see another conflict upon this scale. But when we are all three dead and gone another generation of predators will have grown up. With the speed in the advance of modern science, especially that connected with destruction, any future conflict may well be the last, assuming that any one or anything remains upon this planet. Oh, by the way, Watson, I would be obliged if you would refrain from quoting this outburst of mine, at least during my lifetime!'